Ragged Alice

ALSO BY GARETH L. POWELL

RAGGED ALICE

GARETH L. POWELL

A TOM DOHERTY ASSOCIATES BOOK

NEW YORK

RAGGED ALICE

Cover photo by Andrew Davis/Trevillion Images
Cover design by Fort

Edited by Lee Harris

A Tor.com Book
Published by Tom Doherty Associates
175 Fifth Avenue
New York, NY 10010

www.tor.com

Tor® is a registered trademark of
Macmillan Publishing Group, LLC.

ISBN 978-1-250-22017-2 (ebook)
ISBN 978-1-250-22018-9 (trade paperback)

First Edition: April 2019

Benthyg dros amser byr yw popeth a geir yn y byd hwn.

—Welsh proverb

What dies does not pass out of the universe.

—Marcus Aurelius

Ragged Alice

PROLOGUE

AFTER BEING HIT BY THE CAR, Lisa managed to open her eyes three times before she died.

The first time, she found herself with her cheek pressed against the wet surface of the road. Her feet were resting in the undergrowth on the verge. The rain had stopped and the moon threatened to break through the tattered rags of cloud above the valley. Fleetingly, she wondered why she was there. She had no memory of lying down. The last thing she remembered, she had been walking home, arms folded tightly across her chest, resenting her uncomfortable heels, cursing Daryl for being such an idiot, and cursing herself for having stormed out of the pub instead of demanding to be driven home.

The car stood in the road a dozen or so metres ahead of her. The reflection of its red brake lights seemed to sizzle on the slick tarmac. The engine clicked and pinged as it started to cool.

Maybe whoever was in the car would know why she had chosen to rest here, halfway between the pub on the main road and the town down at the far end of the valley?

She tried to lift her head, but her neck hurt, and she didn't seem to be able to stay awake.

. . .

The second time she opened her eyelids, she had been bundled onto her back, and overfamiliar hands were rifling through the pockets of her coat. Her nose wrinkled at the smell of aftershave and sour lager.

"Daryl?"

The hands stopped their rummaging. Carefully, Daryl extracted her mobile phone, turned it off, and slipped it into his jeans.

"Sorry, love."

"What happened?"

"A bit of an accident." He sounded apologetic. Not angry, like he had been earlier.

"Take me home."

"I can't." He stood and wiped his hands on the oil-stained thighs of his jeans.

"Why not?" She couldn't understand why he wasn't helping her.

"You're hurt proper badly. I'm sorry."

"Why are you sorry?"

He shrugged and looked away, into the darkness.

"I just am, okay."

• • •

When Lisa pried open her eyes for the third and final time, the car had gone, and the air felt fresher. Now she could smell wet earth and wild garlic. The terraced, slate-roofed lights of Pontyrhudd glittered at the end of the valley. A plane passed overhead at high altitude, its vapour trail drawn like a pale spider's thread against the hard, bright stars. Somewhere across the fields, an owl cried.

Her breaths came in slow and shallow sips. Her chest felt full of gauze. Why had Daryl abandoned her out here? As kids, they'd never have ventured this far up the valley, especially at night. Even when they became teenagers, they took their nocturnal backseat passions to the headland overlooking the sea, instinctively distrusting the inland lay-bys and farm tracks. A girl had been murdered up here once, among the gorse and bracken. That was all they needed to know. And with the whole of Wales pressing at their backs, it was sometimes easier to stare west across the Atlantic and picture a distant, attainable liberation somewhere beyond the knife-sharp horizon.

Lisa and Daryl had often talked of going to America. If they ever managed to save up enough money, they were going to hire a Winnebago and drive from New York to

Chicago, and then on along Route 66 to Los Angeles and San Francisco.

At least, that had been the dream. Not that either of them had ever earned enough to put any money aside for such things. Her wages from the hair salon barely covered her rent and bills, and he earned next to nothing as an apprentice mechanic. And now she was pregnant. That was what they had been arguing about: money and timing. That was why she had stormed out and tried to walk the four miles down the valley, from the main road to the town.

Now Daryl was gone, and she was here by herself. She wanted to cry, but the tears wouldn't come. Blood roared in her ears like the ebb of waves on a shingle beach. The fingers of her left hand twitched as nerves fired like loose electrical connections.

And suddenly, she had the prickly sensation she wasn't alone. Her eyes were guttering like expiring candles, but she had the impression that a figure sat cross-legged on the tarmac beside her. A cold hand pressed to her cheek, and she heard the rustle of cloth. Caught a movement like the twitch of a crow's wing or the flick of a ragged cape.

Heard the hiss of a long, indrawn breath.

A voice that whispered to her as she died.

1.

BY THE TIME DCI Holly Craig pulled up at the scene, the local police had closed the road and placed a tent over the body. The last traces of the night's rain had blown inland on a stiff southwesterly, leaving a sky that looked spotless and freshly scrubbed. Flecks of sunlight danced on azure waves. Gorse flowers shivered in the wind.

She closed the car door and curled her lip. She hadn't been back to Pontyrhudd in fifteen years. And she hadn't had a drink in almost six hours.

"Okay, what have we got?"

A plain-clothed young man detached himself from a small knot of uniformed officers.

"Are you the new guvnor?"

"For now."

He looked her up and down, taking in her long auburn hair and army surplus coat.

"Looks like a hit-and-run," he said hesitantly, obviously taken aback by her appearance. He must have been all of twenty-five years old. Pretty enough, but practically a child. His soul looked depressingly untarnished. "The victim's a local girl, Lisa Hughes. Works in the salon."

Holly pulled back a tent flap and glanced at the body. "Drunk driver?"

"Could be."

She let the flap fall shut. "What's your name, son?"

The kid bristled at her tone. "Scott," he said. "Scott Fowler. Detective Sergeant."

Holly smiled. A twitch of the lips. A couple of hundred feet below, a stream wound across the boggy valley floor like a vein of silver winding through slate.

"So, you reckon this was an accident?"

"I think so."

Holly rolled her eyes. She turned on her heel and walked up the road. It was a simple two-lane blacktop that connected Pontyrhudd with the A487, which swept down from Aberystwyth in the north to Fishguard in the south. It was the only way in and out of the town.

"He tapped his brakes here," she said, pointing to a smudge on the surface. "Then again here."

Scott pulled his phone out. He snapped pictures of the marks as she pointed them out. When she reached the bend, she stopped.

"He must have first seen her from here," she said. She closed one eye and held her thumb out at arm's length, lining up the car's trajectory. "Then he touched the brakes again and swerved right, and clipped her *there*."

She pointed to a spot where tyre tracks had chewed up a patch of muddy verge.

Scott dutifully snapped each of the sites as she indicated them.

"So, not an accident, then?"

"No." She returned to her contemplation of the curve, visualising the car's path, the squeal of tyres and the thump of impact.

"This must have been premeditated," she said at length. "There's no way the driver would have had time to decide to run someone over. He had to have been already looking for her when he came around that bend."

Scott lowered his phone. "And there's definitely no way this could have been an accident? Maybe he lost control at the corner there, and overcorrected?"

Holly shook her head. "Just at the spot where our victim happened to be walking? No, I don't buy it. It's too much of a coincidence." She paused to listen as the breeze stirred the planted ranks of fir covering the north side of the valley. A wind turbine stood against the horizon, its blades turning with an insolent disregard for earthly matters. She stuffed her hands into the pockets of her RAF greatcoat. The breeze ruffled her hair.

"Does the victim have a family?"

Scott consulted his notes. "There's a sister, down in the town. We sent a liaison officer down to talk to her."

"When was this?"

"About an hour ago."

"Then it's high time we paid our respects."

. . .

They took the road downhill, following the contours of the valley as it descended towards the sea. Holly's car was a hired Ford. She'd picked it up when she arrived in Carmarthen. There hadn't been time for the local office to assign her an official ride.

Scott sat in the passenger seat, gripping the grab handle above the door window. He was a nervous passenger. But she'd driven this road a thousand times in her youth. She knew every twist and kink, every dip and turn. Every sheep-short pasture, friable stone wall and crooked, black-limbed tree.

Fifteen years, and nothing had changed.

She downshifted into fourth as they came into the town.

Pontyrhudd had never really made it as a tourist destination. It couldn't compete with Aberystwyth, which had a direct connection to Birmingham New Street and the rest of the National Rail network. And with the main road four miles inland, the town saw little in the way of passing trade. Terraced streets barnacled the bracken-topped hills. Shabby cafés and run-down guesthouses adorned the seafront, their windows flecked with the dried salt spray from decades of winter squalls.

It was the kind of town in which rifts and enmities ran beneath everything like festering seams of smouldering peat, and the children in the local primary school stifled beneath the weight of generational feuds stretching back to the misdeeds of their great-grandparents.

When Holly thought of the town, she thought of it in terms of fish fingers and oven chips in front of her grandfather's television, his electric fire lit and his ashtray overflowing with the soggy remains of hand-rolled cigarettes; of her and her friends kicking empty Coke cans on the pavement outside the out-of-season amusement arcades; of enduring endless rainy Sunday afternoons spent looking out from the sash window of her bedroom; and of a general, all-pervading sense of being slowly smothered. So it was strange to see the place again with an outsider's eyes. Once, it had been her whole world. And although she had escaped and moved on, she had somehow been expecting the town to remain as it had been on the day of her departure.

Now, as she followed Scott's directions, she saw that a sort of half-hearted, creeping gentrification had transformed the local cafés into coffee shops and made space on the high street for an art gallery, a tapas restaurant, and a shop selling artisanal bread. Although, having said that, there also seemed to be a lot more charity shops than she remembered, suggesting not everyone had the means to buy into this new aspirational lifestyle.

Some familiar landmarks remained unchanged. Here, she saw the same fish and chip shop where, at the age of fifteen, she'd been taken on her first proper date. There, the bus shelter where she'd broken up with the boy a week later.

Negotiating the narrow streets felt like looking through an album of family photographs, only to find parties unknown had altered some of the pictures—an uncomfortable dissonance between the town she'd carried with her for a decade and a half and the town as it was now.

Still feeling mildly disorientated and unreal, she pulled up at the kerb outside the terraced house owned by Lisa Hughes's sister.

"Okay," she said as she unfastened her seat belt. "Is there anything I should know before I go in there?"

"Like what, guv?"

"If I knew, I wouldn't need to ask."

Scott shrugged.

"I don't think so."

"Does she have a dog?"

"Not as far as I'm aware."

"Good." Holly opened her door. "I don't get on well with dogs."

. . .

Nicola Hughes's house stood a few streets back from the seafront. The window blinds were skew-whiff and the paint on the frames peeling. Holly rapped on the front door and a uniformed police officer answered. She flashed her credentials and was led through to the sitting room, where a tearstained woman sat crying on a sagging futon.

"My name's Detective Chief Inspector Craig," she said. "I'm here to find out why your sister's dead."

The woman looked up in horror and burst into fresh tears.

From the hallway, Scott muttered, "Way to be blunt, guv."

Holly ignored him. She crouched in front of the sobbing woman and put a hand on her arm. She could see the hurt behind the swollen eyes.

"I mean it," she said. "I'm going to find out who did this and prosecute them to the full extent of the law. But first, I'm going to need you to tell me what your sister was doing out on the valley road last night."

Nicola Hughes scrunched and wrung the tissues in her

hands. She sucked in a breath and gave a nod.

"Good," Holly said. "Take your time."

The woman had taken a few knocks over the years, but her internal light still flickered like a stubborn candle.

"She said she was going out with Daryl. Up to the Galleon on the main road."

"Who's Daryl?"

"Her boyfriend. They've been seeing each other for about a year."

"And you don't approve?"

"I've never liked him."

"Any particular reason?"

Nicola's face hardened. "He can get nasty when he's got a drink in him. Proper temper, like."

"Did they argue often?"

"They argued last night. She rang me about ten to eleven in a right old state. Said she'd just walked out on him. I told her to phone a cab, but she wanted to walk home by herself."

Holly glanced at Scott. "Did the victim have a phone on her?" Nobody had mentioned one.

Scott consulted his notepad.

"No, guv."

"Interesting." She turned back to Lisa's sister and asked, "Does Daryl have a surname?"

• • •

Daryl Allen wasn't at home, and nobody at the garage where he worked had seen him since the previous day. So Holly and Scott drove back up the valley, passing the crime scene, and continued on until they reached the junction with the A487.

The Galleon Inn nestled in the crook of the junction. The stones in its walls had been quarried from the local hills, the blackened timbers in its frame taken from an eighteenth-century shipwreck. Its front door faced the road and the fields beyond. From its topmost rear windows, you could see the sea.

Holly parked at the side of the building and sat for a moment, gripping the steering wheel. The Galleon had always been the place the town's young people went. Its proximity to the main road gave it a liminal, edge-of-the-world feel, and as long as you looked vaguely of age, you could always get served. Looking at the chalkboards advertising happy hours and meal deals to passing motorists, she felt a sudden queasy nostalgia. This had been the place she'd first learned to drink.

"Are you all right, guv?"

"I'm fine."

The last thing she needed to think about right now was alcohol. She climbed out of the car and sniffed the air. A truck thundered past. She could do this. She really could.

"Come on."

She strode around to the front of the building and pushed through the thick oak door. Scott hurried to keep up.

Inside, the place was exactly what you would have expected: nautical paraphernalia on the walls, a fruit machine cycling in the corner. The wooden panelling on the walls bore a couple of decades' worth of accumulated scuffs and scratches, and the ceiling glowered the yellow-ivory colour of nicotine-stained teeth. A brass rail ran around the bar, and the pumps bore the colourful logos of independent breweries—tiny paintings of goblins, pirate ships and foxes. A giant wall-mounted flat-screen TV showed a rolling news channel.

As Holly stepped into the gloom of the public bar, the barmaid called, "We're not open yet."

Holly put her hands in the pockets of her long coat and walked slowly to the counter, letting her eyes adjust to the stale gloom.

"I don't care. I'm here to ask questions."

The barmaid stopped setting up and gave her a look. "Are you the police?"

"Show her your warrant card, Scott."

"Yes, guv."

Holly waited while Scott fumbled his wallet from the

inside pocket of his suit jacket. In her experience, 90 percent of the British public had no idea what a real police ID looked like, but it always helped to flash one. It provided a framework for discussion.

"Did you hear about the girl who got run over last night?"

The barmaid gave a cautious nod. The light inside her skull was bright but blemished. She'd done things she couldn't have been proud of.

"Yeah, I passed the police cars on my way up here this morning."

"Did you know her?"

"Not personal, like."

"But you'd recognise her?"

The girl gave a shrug. "Lisa Hughes? Sure. She was in here last night."

Holly propped her elbows on the bar and leant forwards, trying to ignore the way the light glinted off the half-empty bottle of single malt on the shelf behind the bar.

"Who was she with?"

"Her boyfriend."

"Daryl Allen?"

"Yeah. His dad owns the garage in town."

"How did they seem?"

Another shrug. "Oh, you know. Not happy. They had a

few drinks and a bit of an argument."

"Violent?"

The barmaid shook her head. "No, nothing like that. Just, you know, words. Then she barged out."

"And Daryl followed her?"

"No, he had another drink first."

"What was he drinking?" Holly's eyes strayed back to that bottle of whiskey in its shaft of sunlight.

"Lager."

"And her?"

"Pineapple juice, I think."

"And then he went after her?"

For the first time, the girl behind the bar looked worried. She didn't want to get anybody into trouble. "I don't know. He left about fifteen minutes after she did."

"And he was driving?"

"Yeah . . ."

"Thank you."

Holly turned on her heel and left the way she'd entered. As soon as she was outside, she closed her eyes and inhaled, savouring the smells of warm tarmac and wild hedge flowers. It felt as if she'd been holding her breath the entire time she'd been inside. By the time Scott caught up with her, she'd regained her composure.

"Well," she said. "This all seems pretty straightforward."

"Guv?"

She straightened up. "Lisa and Daryl argued. She walked out and he had another drink. Then he went after her."

Scott mulled it over. "That would have given her enough time to walk as far as she did," he said.

"He was angry and drunk. He went after her with the only weapon he had at his disposal."

"His car."

"Bingo."

She scuffed the toe of her boot in the gravel at the edge of the road. She could already hear her new apartment in Carmarthen calling to her.

"Put out an APB for Daryl," she said.

2.

HOLLY HAD A ROOM booked in the Royal Hotel on the seafront. It was the kind of hotel whose corridors you could imagine being stalked by disappointed Victorian ghosts. She hadn't bothered unpacking. With luck, she hoped to be out of there and on the road back to Carmarthen as soon as Daryl Allen confessed to intentionally hitting Lisa Hughes with his car. While they waited for the uniforms to locate the young man, she and Scott took a break in the Royal Hotel's front bar. Scott took his coffee black, with no sweeteners, while Holly had her tea heaped with enough sugar to support a modest plantation. Across the street, waves rushed and hissed over pebbles. Gulls wheeled in the air.

"So," Scott said. "Do you think the boyfriend did it?"

"With any luck." Holly stirred her tea and placed the spoon on the edge of her saucer. A carriage clock ticked on the mantelpiece.

Scott chewed his bottom lip. When he finally spoke, he said, "Can I ask you something?"

"Sure."

"Have I done something to piss you off?"

Holly raised her eyebrows.

"No, not at all."

"Are you sure?" He scratched his cheek, not quite meeting her eyes. "Because I was starting to wonder."

Holly glanced out at a pair of elderly women in headscarves and raincoats dragging their wheeled shopping baskets along the front. She could have snapped back a one-liner, but it would have been like kicking a Labrador. Scott was young and keen. His suit wasn't expensive, but it was clean and pressed. His hair was smart without being overtly stylish, and his fingernails were neat and dirt-free. His build suggested he played sports, but his complexion suggested he tended to avoid the alcoholic binges that tended to follow team matches. If she had to come up with two words to describe him, she'd probably go for *honest* and *ambitious*.

"I'm sorry," she said, feeling something unwind in her chest. "I don't mean to be short with you. It's just strange being back here again."

Scott looked relieved. "How long has it been?" he asked.

"Fifteen years, give or take a couple of months. I went away to college in London and never came back."

"Do you still have family here?"

The question was well intentioned, but hurt. Holly

clasped her hands. "No, not anymore." She let out a breath. "My mam died when I was a baby. My dad went into a spiral. Gave up on everything, including me. Died a couple of years later."

"I'm sorry, I shouldn't pry."

Holly shrugged. "You're a detective. You like to know people's stories. It comes with the job."

Scott's cheeks reddened. "I guess I was curious."

"To find out why I requested the transfer back here to Dyfed-Powys?"

"Yes, guv."

Holly sucked air through her teeth. Through the window, she watched the flags flap on the promenade.

"There was an incident in a school," she said, not looking in his direction. "It didn't end well. And after that, I decided I wanted to get away from the city for a while."

In fact, she hadn't slept properly in six months. Not since the day a recently laid-off teacher named Ben Clarke walked back into the school where his ex-girlfriend still worked as a secretary. He'd been wearing a black baseball cap and a white T-shirt. He'd also been carrying a pistol and a carving knife. During the resulting standoff, he'd killed two teachers, the girlfriend, and three students before finally turning the gun on himself. Holly remembered each and every one of their names and faces. During the train journey from Paddington to Carmarthen, she'd had time to run through the list at least a hundred times.

"Ah." Scott fiddled with his teaspoon. "I'm sorry, guv."

"These things happen." She heaved out a sigh. "So, tell me about yourself. What brings you to Pontyrhudd?"

Scott leant back in his chair. His eyes were the same colour as the sea, his hair the colour of sand.

"There's not much to tell." He said it with an easy smile. "My family comes from just up the road, in Llanfarian. I went to university in Aberystwyth and then joined the force."

"Are you married?"

"Yeah, twelve months now."

"Kids?"

"Not yet. You?"

Holly clicked her tongue. "No serious relationships."

"Because of the job?"

"Partly." They were getting onto dangerous ground now. With one finger, she scraped her coffee cup around until the handle faced the other way. Then turned it back again. "I just never found anyone I could trust."

And she probably never would. How could she truly trust anyone when she might at any instant glimpse their inner darkness and their sins dragging behind them like Marley's chains?

She snatched up her cup and inhaled the steam. In the kitchen, she could hear the chef rattling pots and pans on the hob. The smell of frying onions crept under the door. Her eyes flicked to the carriage clock above the fireplace. Only eleven thirty. She desperately wanted a whiskey and it wasn't even lunchtime yet.

"That's an interesting coat you've got there," Scott said. "Is it army surplus?"

Appreciating the change of subject, Holly looked down at the grey lapels and brass buttons.

"Royal Air Force," she said. "It belonged to my grandfather. He said it brought him luck."

Scott looked thoughtful. But before he could ask any more questions, his phone buzzed. He held it to his ear and listened for a few seconds before saying, "Thanks, we'll be right there."

He pocketed the phone and turned to her with a strange expression on his face.

"Have they found Daryl?"

"Yes."

"Are they bringing him in?"

"Not as such." Scott scraped back on his chair. "We . . . we have to go to him."

Holly frowned. She'd had more than enough chasing around for one morning. All she wanted was to get the little scumbag in a cell so she could go home and sink into a hot bath with a bottle of Jack.

"Why?"

Scott stood. He rubbed his jaw as if not quite able to believe what he was about to say. Holly resisted the urge to grab him by the collar and shake it out of him. After a moment, he looked at her.

"He's been murdered."

3.

PONTYRHUDD STOOD AT THE end of the valley, where the waters of the River Rhudd surrendered themselves to the heave and crash of the Atlantic Ocean. Linked by a fingernail-shaped stretch of pebbled beach, the steep, bracken-strewn sides of the *cwm* continued out into the surf for a few hundred yards, forming bracken-strewn headlands that tapered into the waves like the petrified tails of sleeping dragons.

The headland to the north had a steep path leading up from the end of the concourse to a small chapel overlooking the town. Holly and Scott were met at the top of the path by a uniformed constable in his midthirties.

"Where is he?" she asked.

"Over here, ma'am." The constable led them through the ranks of forgotten, lichen-crusted graves to a marker near the back of the graveyard. As they approached, Holly could see a pair of legs protruding from behind the drunkenly leaning stone.

"Best you brace yourselves," the constable said, removing his cap and dabbing at his forehead with a folded handkerchief. His soul looked tired and grubby. The wind toyed with his thin sandy hair.

Scott made a face.

"Gruesome, is it?"

"About as gruesome as it gets, sir."

"Okay, thanks, Perkins. We'll take it from here."

"Very good, sir."

Looking relieved, Constable Perkins replaced his cap and resumed his post at the top of the path, ready to deter inquisitive dog walkers.

From up here, you could see the whole town, and much of the sweep of Cardigan Bay, the 150-mile crescent-shaped bite that defined the western coast of Wales, from Bardsey Island in the north to Strumble Head in the south. Local legend had it that on a clear day you could even glimpse the coastline of Wexford in Ireland—but as Wexford lay more than a hundred miles to the west, Holly strongly doubted the truth of that particular tradition.

Her coat flapped around her legs.

"Are you ready?" she said.

Scott's hands fidgeted at his sides. He blew air through his cheeks. He was trying to be brave and nonchalant but couldn't disguise his nerves.

"Yeah," he said. "Let's do it."

They stepped forward together.

Daryl lay spread-eagled on the grass. The handle of a knife protruded from his heart. The top of his head pressed against the worn gravestone. His hands lay at his sides, palms turned upwards. His shirt had been pushed up and his belly slit from hip to hip, exposing greasy blue ropes of intestine. Holly could see where the gulls had tried to pull some free. But the thing that disturbed her most was the state of his eyes. Twigs jutted from the sockets like cigarette ends extinguished in broken egg yolks. They stood without speaking for a minute or so. There wasn't much to say. The breeze continued to blow in off the sea. Seagulls cried like hungry mourners.

Eventually, Scott swore under his breath and turned away.

Holly swallowed her disquiet and crouched by the body. The gaping stomach wound smelled like a butcher's window display. Flies came and went. She ignored all that and concentrated on the man's disfigured face. Occasionally, something lingered after death. The whole body didn't shut down at once. And sometimes, even with the brain flatlined and the heart stopped, there might still be a fading spark behind those ruined eyes.

Fighting back her revulsion, she reached out and pressed her fingers and thumb to the dead man's wind-chilled temples.

Daryl Allen wore a white T-shirt, stained blue jeans

and a black bomber jacket. His hair had been shaved into neat rows, and he had a gold stud in his nose.

"Come on," she muttered. She closed her eyes and tried to clear her mind. But all she could hear were the wind and waves. If any flickering residue of the young mechanic's humanity remained, it had degraded too far for her to parse.

4.

DESPITE THE MISGIVINGS OF the hotel's owners, Holly commandeered the hotel's business suite. She needed somewhere to set up her incident room, and that seemed as good a place as any. Despite its inherent shabbiness, the hotel was situated in the heart of town and had reasonably decent Wi-Fi and passable tea and coffee facilities. She laid claim to the whiteboard that had been screwed to the wall at one end of the room. This would be the focus of her investigation—the master record of her thought processes. The rest of the space was given over to cheap Ikea desks and folding chairs, which would serve as workstations for the rest of her staff.

In addition to Scott Fowler, she now had an office manager, responsible for the smooth running of the investigation; an enquiry team, made up of three uniforms and two CID officers; a scientific services manager, in charge of the gathering of forensic evidence; and an exhibits officer, whose job it was to bag and label every fragment of evidence. Aside from DS Fowler and Constable Perkins, she didn't know any of them personally. She hadn't been here long enough. But they all came recommended by her senior officers at HQ in Carmarthen—and for now, that would have to be enough.

Their first assembly took place at six in the afternoon. It had taken that long to gather them all together. Briefly, Holly laid out the circumstances of the case as she saw them.

"A pair of young lovers argue," she said. "The girlfriend storms out. Fifteen minutes later, the boyfriend goes after her. He has a temper and several drinks inside him. He hits her with his car and leaves her to die." She held up an evidence bag. "We found Lisa's missing mobile phone in Daryl's jacket pocket, which places him at the scene."

"Why do you think he took the phone?" asked one of the uniformed officers. His name was Morgan, and he was built like a partially shaved bear.

"Daryl knew she was dying," Holly answered. "He couldn't bring himself to finish her off, so he left her there. But he took her phone because he didn't want her calling for help."

"What a bastard." Morgan flexed his big hands, as if wishing he could have wrapped them around the kid's windpipe. Beside him, Perkins gave a snort.

"I reckon whoever killed him did the world a favour."

He wiped a stray lick of sandy hair over his poorly con-cealed bald spot.

Holly rapped a knuckle against the whiteboard.

"You've seen these photos. They didn't just kill him. They slit him open and poked out his eyes and stabbed him in the heart. To me, that looks an awful lot like a re-venge killing.

"I want you to check Lisa Hughes's friends and family," she said. "Find out if any of them might have had the means and opportunity to do this."

. . .

As the rest of the team filed out, Scott joined her at the whiteboard. She tapped a fingernail against her teeth.

"I figure Daryl must have been killed by someone he knew," she told him. "Someone he arranged to meet in the graveyard. I can't imagine anyone dragging a corpse all the way up there in broad daylight without being seen."

Scott loosened his tie. It bore a rugby club emblem. Judging by his build, Holly guessed he'd been a fly-half, or maybe even a winger. He looked as if he could move quickly when he needed to.

"Trouble is, guv," he said, "in a place like this, every-body knows everybody else. And word got around fast about Lisa Hughes. Almost anyone could have done it."

Holly considered this. Despite her hopes for a quick resolution, it seemed she would be stuck in Pontyrhudd for the duration. From the corner of her eye, she caught Scott sneaking a glance at his watch.

"Do you need to go?" she asked.

He gave a guilty start. "I was on the early shift," he said. "And the wife's on nights at the hospital. I'd like to get home and see her before she goes to work, if that's okay with you, guv?"

Holly pursed her lips. Sometimes she forgot her colleagues had personal lives beyond the confines of their jobs.

"Go," she said. "Get some rest. Be back here first thing tomorrow."

He smiled. "Thanks, guv. *Nos da.*"

And with that, he was gone, leaving her standing alone in an empty room, in an out-of-season seaside hotel.

For half an hour, she continued to stare at the photos of Daryl Allen, but however hard she scrutinized them, she remained no closer to a revelation regarding the identity of his killer. Finally, with a sigh, she decided to call it a day. The hotel bar was in the next room, and she was long overdue a drink. She turned out the lights and walked through.

The bar featured a large bay window that looked out over the sea. The sun was lowering towards the horizon.

This early in the evening, no other drinkers were in evidence. A handwritten note on the cash register instructed her to ring a bell for service.

When she pressed the buzzer, the receptionist came through from the desk out front. She was a young lady with half-moon spectacles and a glass eye. The name tag pinned to her blouse said SYLVIA. Holly tried not to stare but couldn't help noticing the colour of the glass eye didn't match the real one.

"What can I get you, Officer?"

"A double Jack Daniel's, please." She pulled out a ten-pound note, but the girl waved it away.

"We'll put it on your room," she said. She turned and filled a glass from the row of optics on the back wall. Packs of peanuts and bags of pork scratching hung from promotional cards. Pickled eggs bobbed in a glass jar.

"You were looking at my eye," she said over her shoulder.

Holly winced. "I'm sorry, I didn't mean any offence."

"Oh, that's quite all right." The girl seemed airy and unconcerned. "Everybody knows about it." She plonked the glass on the counter between them. "Some say it's lucky. Do you want ice?"

"No thanks."

Holly reached for her drink and raised it in salute. "*Iechyd da,*" she said. But before she could take a sip,

Sylvia clamped a restraining hand on her forearm.

"I expect you're wondering why it's a different colour to my good eye, though, aren't you?" Her fingers felt like steel wires.

"Um, not really."

"It was my great-grandfather's." The girl leaned closer and lowered her voice. The light darkened behind her eyes. "It's more than a hundred years old, and it's seen a lot, this eye. It could tell you some tales."

Holly resisted the urge to pull away. "Is that right?"

Sylvia shuddered. She stood transfixed, jaw clenched and grip firm on Holly's forearm.

"Secret things," she breathed. "Things that happened in the woods."

A car went past outside. The clock chimed. A log spat and crackled in the grate. And then suddenly Sylvia blinked and jerked upright again.

"I'm sorry," she said, smiling. "What were we talking about? You wanted ice, didn't you?"

• • •

Amy Lao leant back in her chair and glanced out of the office window. She had spent the evening working on a puff piece for the local rag. Thirty years ago, a UFO flap had gripped Pontyrhudd. Fourteen children at the local primary school claimed to have seen a flying saucer in the field beside their school, and when the headmaster asked them to draw the craft, the pictures they produced all bore a striking similarity. Now, on the anniversary of the event, she was filling space in the paper by reprinting some of the photos and statements from the children—many of whom still lived in the town.

It was fair to say her journalistic career hadn't worked out the way she'd hoped it might. When she'd left university, she'd expected that by now she'd be working for the BBC. Instead, she was stuck here, in the arse-end of nowhere, writing up town council meetings and court reports to fill the gaps between the paid adverts that formed the local paper's true content. She missed the bustle of her native Birmingham. She was a city girl at heart, and Pontyrhudd, while affording some stunning coastal sunsets, couldn't really compete with the churning vitality of Britain's second-largest city.

In fact, she was about to pack up for the night and head home to her bedsit when her mobile rang.

"Hello, Amy, it's Neil. Neil Perkins."

Neil Perkins was one of the local constables. She'd interviewed him last month, when a load of Rees Thomas's cows had got loose on the main road and caused a four-mile tailback before they could be persuaded back to their field.

"What can I do for you, Neil?"

"It's more what I can do for you, Amy love. I've got a tip-off, see."

Amy pulled her spiral-topped notebook towards her and picked up a pen. Maybe the cows had escaped again. "This had better be good."

"Oh, it is."

She clicked the pen. "What is it?"

"It seems we've got a double murder. Lisa Hughes got knocked down on the valley road last night, and now her boyfriend's shown up in the chapel grounds with his belly cut open and bloody sticks in his eyes."

"Christ."

"I was the first to see the body. Proper horrible it was."

"I don't doubt it." She jotted the names of the victims on her pad. "So, what's happening about it?"

"There's a new DCI down from London. She's heading up the investigation."

"What's her name?"

"Craig."

Amy smiled. "Is that her first name or her surname?"

"I think she's Dai Craig's granddaughter."

"Dai Craig?"

"Before your time, love. His daughter was murdered, and he brought the girl up. Until the kid fucked off to London, anyhow."

"And now she's back?"

"Looks that way."

"Where's she staying, Neil?"

"Down the Royal."

"Cheers, pet."

"You're welcome, like. Just make sure this time you spell my name right."

5.

AFTER A RESTLESS NIGHT, Holly woke at seven the following morning. The sheets smelled wrong. The pillows were too soft. She had left her window open and could hear the waves rustling up the beach and the gulls keening on the wind. And, in that dazed state between sleep and realization, when the boundary between the two seemed porous and negotiable, she felt as if she'd never left Pontyrhudd—as if those fifteen years in London had been no more than lingering wisps of sea mist dispersed by the rising sun.

Here she was. Thirty-two years old, still single, unforgiving, remote and difficult to get along with—more a product of her father and this town than she would ever have cared to admit.

Somewhere along the way, she realised, she'd stopped thinking of herself as a person with a past. In her head, she'd been DCI Craig for five years now. She might find it hard to relate to her coworkers, but she was good at her job. It had come to define her. Everything else was just baggage she didn't need.

Of course, being cranky, reserved and often hungover hadn't endeared her to her colleagues in the Met. She certainly wouldn't have risen as high as she had if her record for solving cases hadn't been exemplary. Social niceties were one thing, but results spoke for themselves. While the bosses may have been disappointed the day she left London, she was sure the rest of her team had thrown a party. They had thought she couldn't see them smirking behind their computer monitors as she called out her good-byes.

Reluctantly, she pulled aside the sheet and slid out of bed. An empty bottle lay on the carpet. She walked around the room in bare feet, opening drawers and cupboards to see what they contained. She flicked through the available TV channels and found a local news report on Lisa Hughes. It was just a shot of the white tent that covered the scene, followed by an old school photo of the deceased. No real information at all.

Leaving the TV playing in the background, she went for a shower. In the bathroom, the hair products were stacked in sideways orange crates that had been nailed together to form a set of shelves. One shelf for shampoos, another for conditioners, a third for gels and waxes. The shower was one of those walk-in arrangements with slate tiles and an incomprehensibly complex nozzle. She rinsed herself off as best she could and picked some clothes from the wardrobe, eventually settling on a simple combination of blue jeans and black T-shirt.

When Scott arrived at the hotel at eight, he found her sitting on the bench outside, wrapped in her RAF coat and sipping tea from a cup and saucer.

For her, tea was the one truly pure and necessary thing on this miserable earth, and the favourite and most worthwhile of her vices.

"Morning, guv." He handed her a folded newspaper. "I see we made the local rag."

Holly dropped it onto the bench beside her without bothering to glance at the headline. "And a fat lot of good that's going to do us."

Scott grimaced at her tone. "With respect, guv, there's something here you ought to see."

"What?"

He opened the paper and stepped back. Holly frowned at him and then down at the black-and-white photograph on page two.

It was a portrait of her mother, aged twenty-one. She had shaggy, dyed-brown hair and thickly applied eyeliner and was wearing a cardigan over a long-sleeved black polo neck. She looked kind of like the emo girl in *The Breakfast Club*, before the disastrous makeover.

"What the fuck is this?"

Scott's Adam's apple bobbed. "According to this, Daryl

Allen's injuries were identical to the ones found on your mother's body."

Holly's stomach clenched like a fist. She had only been a couple of weeks old at the time of her mother's murder. "Is it true?" She'd heard grisly rumours from her classmates but assumed them to be exaggerations.

"I've asked one of the uniforms to dig out the file." Scott bit his lower lip. "Look, I'm sorry. I didn't mean to—"

Holly became aware the cup and saucer were rattling in her hand. She put them down on the arm of the bench and rose to her feet.

"I think I need a walk," she said.

Without waiting for an answer, she strode across the road. By the time Scott caught up with her, she was standing at the water's edge, hands thrust deeply into the pockets of her airman's coat, her hair straggling out behind her.

"I was a baby," she said. Her eyes were fixed on the horizon. "Nobody told me anything. I didn't even know she'd been murdered until I went to school and heard the other kids talking."

She kicked a pebble into the surf.

"After my dad died, my grandfather took me in. I always got the impression he didn't approve of my mother. That maybe he thought my mother somehow deserved what she got."

"I'm sorry, guv."

Holly watched another wave roll up the beach.

"He used to bring me down here all the time. I'd spend hours throwing stones into the sea and make a wish every time I did. But then he'd tap out his pipe and say it didn't matter how many rocks I threw, the tide would always bring them back."

She eyed a tangle of driftwood and fishing line. "I joined the police because of her," she said. "But I never looked into her death. I never found out the specifics. I mean, she was *dead*. I guess I didn't think it was relevant."

"Seems it's relevant now."

Holly clenched her fists inside the pockets of her coat. "No shit."

Her head hurt from last night's whiskey. All she wanted was to fall in a heap on the tide-slicked shingle and let the world do what it would, without her input or involvement. And she would have done if there hadn't been a stubborn professional streak that refused to let her give up so easily—a queasy stirring that drove her to remain standing and demanded she march back into that hotel, grab another cup of tea and set her team about the task of solving these crimes.

"Do me a favour," she said.

"Anything."

"Don't mention this to anyone." She took a deep

breath and let it out into the face of the offshore wind. "I mean it." For the first time, she turned to look at him. "It was a long time ago. If they get a sniff of any of this, and realise that's my ma, they'll pull me off the case."

Scott pursed his lips. He put his hands in his pockets. "I can't promise anything."

"What do you mean?" She'd guessed he was ambitious, but would he really throw her under the bus to further his own career? She hadn't pegged him as disloyal, but they hardly knew each other, and she hadn't taken the time to find out where his allegiances lay.

The young man looked down at his shoes. "Listen," he said. "I respect the chain of command and all that *cachu*. And you seem to know what you're about, so I'm not going to say anything." He glanced up. "But if I think you're compromising this investigation, even for a second, I can't promise not to report you."

His honesty felt like an overdue splash of cold water. Holly rocked back on her heels. "Fair enough," she said.

Scott inclined his head. "So long as we understand each other."

Holly thought about it. Then she peeled off her fingerless gloves. "My name's Holly," she said, holding out her right hand.

Scott looked down at it. Then he smiled and took it in his. "Scott," he said. "But I believe I already told you that."

"I believe you did."

They both smiled. Then Holly let go and returned her hand to her coat pocket, and they went back to being two people standing on a beach.

"Shall we get back to work?" she asked.

He looked up and down the line of surf and then gave her a relieved grin. "Yes," he said. "Let's."

Side by side, they walked back across the road. As they entered the incident room, they were confronted by one of the CID officers. His name was Ralph Potts. Three days' worth of stubble peppered his double chin. Yellow nicotine stains discoloured the middle finger of his right hand.

"Guv," he said in a gruff Valleys accent, "thank Christ you're here. We've got another body."

6.

THE BUTCHER'S SHOP SAT on the high street, nestled between a tattoo parlour and a charity shop. It was one of those traditional shops that had been in the same family for at least three generations. The shop front and much of the inside were heavily tiled. The window would usually have featured trays of sausages, steaks, bacon rashers, chops and black puddings, but there was no meat on display this morning. The circling flies seemed puzzled by its absence. The dog on the stoop whined as Holly stepped over it.

Inside, the place had the air of a slaughterhouse. The smell seemed to creep past the hand she held over her mouth and nose. It tugged at the back of her throat, insinuated itself into the lining of her nose. Behind the counter, blood had run into all the seams between the tiles, forming an obscene city map. The corpse lay at the centre.

"Who is he?"

"His name's Mike Owen, guv." Potts scratched his belly. "He's the owner's kid."

"Who's the owner?"

"Owen the meat."

"Of course it is. Any connection between this victim and the other two?"

"Aside from the way he's laid out, there's none I can see."

Holly pursed her lips. Mike Owen had been killed in the same manner as Daryl Allen. His apron had been torn aside and his stomach slit. Kebab skewers had been driven so far into his eyes the points were touching the bone at the back of his skull.

Had her mother really been killed like this? She clenched her jaw and squeezed her fists to stop herself shuddering at the thought. In the face of such atrocity, it was small wonder her father had collapsed in on himself. For the first time in years, she felt her resentment lessen a notch.

"Who was first on the scene?" she asked.

"Perkins again."

"Did he see anyone else?"

"No." Potts seemed almost to be enjoying himself. "He says he found him like this."

Holly waved a hand in front of her face, trying to waft aside the smell. It wasn't unusual for a corpse to void its bowels, but young Mike seemed to have done so with a particular curry-fuelled enthusiasm that would have startled even the most seasoned undertaker. Beside her, Scott was struggling to conceal his disgust.

"*Ach-y-fi,*" he said.

On the other side of the body, Potts's smoke-deadened sense of smell seemed to have rendered him immune to the stench. He grinned at their discomfort.

Holly looked around the scene. The knife that had cut the boy's stomach had been taken from a rack at the back of the shop and now lay beside the body; the skewers that had punctured his eyes had been taken from the counter, where other identical skewers waited to be threaded through layers of chicken, lamb and vegetables.

"What do you think? Is this the same killer, or a copycat?" she asked.

Scott rubbed a hand across his mouth.

"It could be a copycat," he said. "The murderer didn't bring tools with him; he used what was at hand."

Holly tapped her chin. "But the killer must have known there would be knives here. Maybe they came here specifically to gather weapons." She looked to Potts. "Check with the owner and see if there are any knives missing."

"Yes, guv."

She took one last look at the scene. The forensic team would pull what they could from the site, but their results could take hours or days to bear fruit. If the killer intended to keep racking up victims at this rate, she couldn't afford to delay.

"But why kill the boy?" Scott asked, following her as she made her way back towards the street. "It doesn't make sense. I can kind of understand someone killing Daryl as revenge for running over the girl, but why the lad? He wasn't involved."

Holly hesitated at the door. "I don't know," she said. "But it's our job to find out."

Outside, a small crowd had gathered to nose. Old women with eyes made of flint and coal, pub regulars with roll-ups dangling from faces hacked out of boiled ham, a gaggle of teenage girls flapping and squawking like seabirds with mobile phones. Constables Walsh and Perkins were doing their level best to hold them back.

As Holly emerged from the butcher's shop, everyone stopped jostling. They looked at her expectantly, and for an instant, she saw herself through their eyes: an obviously hungover big-city cop in scuffed Doc Martens and her granddad's old overcoat, standing next to a smartly turned out local lad nearly a decade younger. She must look like his eccentric aunt. Her in her black T-shirt and jeans, him in a suit and tie. Did any of them recognise her? She'd been gone fifteen years, but there might be some here who remembered her as a girl and might connect the woman she was with the awkward, gangly adolescent she'd once been. She scanned their faces for the school friends who'd dragged her from the river on the day of her accident and was relieved to see they weren't there. If they had been present, she wouldn't have known what to say to them. She owed them her life, but a part of her also resented their intrusion. Had they not risked themselves to save her, she might never have had to shoulder the burden of her gift.

She turned left towards the seafront and began walking. While she had been indoors, ominous clouds had rolled in to eclipse the sun, and the wind brought with it the smell of rain and damp vegetation.

• • •

An old woman waited on the hotel steps. She wore a man's white tuxedo jacket over a lilac ball gown and was smoking a cigarette.

"Are you the detective, love?"

Holly paused. The old girl must have been ninety if she was a day. Her hands looked like sausage skins filled with walnuts. She leant her weight on a silver-topped cane and had slicked back her silver hair with fragrant pomade.

"Can I help you?"

The woman looked her up and down disapprovingly. "I doubt it, *cariad*. I rather thought I might help you."

"This is Mrs. Phillips," Scott said. "She's one of the ho-tel's long-term residents."

Mrs. Phillips ignored him. She brushed the pale grey wool of Holly's sleeve.

"I knew your grandfather," she said. "He was a sweet man."

Holly blinked in surprise. "You did?" Her grandfather had died a year or so back. She remembered most of his friends but had no memory of this woman.

"Oh yes, I knew him *very* well." The old woman's smile revealed false teeth the colour of sun-cracked piano keys. "He always looked very smart in his uniform. In fact, I still see him about the place now and again."

Holly shook her head. "I'm sorry," she said, "but he's dead."

"Oh, I know that, love. But that doesn't mean I can't still see him from time to time."

Her gown rustled as she turned to Scott. "Lovely to see you, Scotty lad. Are you keeping out of trouble?"

Scott smiled. "I'm doing my best, Mrs. Phillips."

"Good boy." She squeezed his hand. "Now, if you'll ex-cuse me, I must be going. I have a lunch date, and I'd like to get there before the rain comes or the young man in-volved changes his mind."

As she tottered onto the pavement, Holly called after her. "Hey, I thought you said you were going to help me?"

Mrs. Phillips paused. She looked back with rheumy eyes the colour of her teeth. "Yes, love. I have a message for you."

"Well?"

"Your grandfather says maybe you should leave this one alone." Her fingertips flicked at the wilting red carnation on the tuxedo's lapel. "And maybe some things are better left buried."

7.

RAIN FELL ACROSS THE bracken-brown hills like a biblical punishment. It dripped from the town's slick slate roofs, overflowed the gutters and ran in gurgling torrents down the steep-sided streets.

DCI Holly Craig stood at the hotel window and looked out at the lifeless grey sea, which this afternoon seemed as beatendown and dejected as everything else in Pontyrhudd. She wondered if Mrs. Phillips had made it to her rendezvous before the onset of the deluge. Despite the crazy old dear's ramblings, she hated to think of that ball gown hanging limp and drenched and that rumpled old face running with washed-out hair oil and mascara. If Ralph Potts's solid build and blunt manner represented the traditional stone and brick terraces of the valley's sides, Mrs. Phillips had to be the living personification of the Victorian buildings on the seafront—their facades once proud and enthusiastic but now washed out, half-forgotten and clinging to past glories, their lungs ravaged by years of smoke, black mould and neglect.

The whiteboard at the far end of the business

suite–cum–incident room had become a tangle of names and arrows. Lisa Hughes, Daryl Allen and Mike Owen. The first two were obviously connected. But who had killed Daryl, and why was Mike dead? And what possible connection could any of it have to a killing that had happened thirty-two years ago?

Offshore, gulls plunged into the somber waters. They dropped like missiles, pitching gouts of white spray into the air where they fell. From this distance, Holly couldn't tell which of them made successful catches. She simply watched as they bobbed up and hauled themselves back into the lowering sky, ready for another dive.

Pontyrhudd wasn't a large place. Somebody in this town must know why Daryl and Mike had been slain in such a grisly fashion. And whoever that person was, they would most likely be the murderer.

The door of the suite opened. Holly turned to see Scott's artfully slicked-back head appear around it.

"Guv, I've got someone who wants to meet you."

Holly rolled her eyes. "Who is it?"

"The reporter from the local rag."

"Tell her I'm busy."

Scott grimaced. "That's going to be kind of hard."

Holly sighed. "She's there with you, isn't she?"

Scott let the door swing fully open. "Yes, guv."

The woman standing behind him only came up to his

shoulder. She wore a thick parka and a woollen hat. Scott waved her into the room and then left with a barely concealed smirk.

"Pleased to meet you, Detective Chief Inspector. My name's Amy Lao."

"What do you want?"

"Oh, you know." Lao shrugged with one shoulder. "Access, comment. That sort of thing." From her accent, Holly guessed she'd been raised in Birmingham.

"I don't have time to be talking to the press."

"Of course not," Lao said. "And for the record, I don't want to talk to you either. I just want to follow you around and get first dibs on any information you might turn up."

The light behind the woman's eyes seemed to dance like a hopeful birthday candle. Holly smiled. She couldn't help it.

"Please explain why you think I'd benefit from having a reporter underfoot?"

"I won't be underfoot," Lao said. "In fact, I might even be useful. After all, I was the one who turned up the connection between these killings and the death of your mother."

Cold fingers closed on Holly's stomach. The smile dropped from her face and she said, "So you know who I am, then?"

Lao smiled. "I'm a reporter. Finding shit out is *literally* my job description."

"I don't want to be taken off this case."

"And you won't be. I won't tell anyone who you are." Lao pantomimed sewing her lips closed. "As long as I get what I need."

"Are you trying to blackmail me?"

"Is it working?"

"Not really."

Lao huffed. "Can we speak honestly?" she asked.

Holly raised an eyebrow. "Please do."

Lao grew serious. "I've done my homework," she said. "I have a contact in the Met and know what your colleagues thought of you. The names they used to call you behind your back. And I know all about your special 'talent.'"

Holly stiffened. "Oh you do, do you?"

The reporter took a step forward. "I'm not here to mock. Honestly. My grandmother in Hong Kong had the exact same thing. She could judge a person just by looking into their eyes. And she was never wrong."

Holly had never heard of anyone else with a disorder like hers. And nobody had ever spoken to her as if they believed her hallucinations might be real. Most people thought she was crazy. Fascinated despite herself, she unfolded her arms.

"Is that true?"

"I swear on my life."

"Did she know what caused it?"

Lao shrugged. "She said it was a trick played on her by the fox spirit."

"I suppose that's as good an explanation as any."

"So, do we have a deal?"

"What kind of deal?" Against her better judgment, Holly found herself warming to the plain-speaking Brummie.

"You let me tag along, and I'll help you solve your mother's murder."

"That's not what I'm investigating."

"But it's clearly linked."

"Fine."

"What does that mean?"

"It means you can stick around. Just don't get in the way, and don't print anything without my say-so."

Amy Lao grinned and thrust out her hand. "Deal!"

Holly hesitated for a second, and then reached out and shook. "I'd better not regret this."

. . .

Holly's next visitor was the mayor. Ieuan Davies was fifty-four years old and had been chair of the local council for as long as anybody could remember. It was mostly a ceremonial position, but she got the impression he took it seriously. He wore a brown suit, a black tie and a double handful of gold rings. His hair was the colour of dirty sand and slicked back at the sides.

"Pleased to meet you, Detective." He was struggling to conceal his surprise at her appearance.

Holly looked down at the thick chain of office draped around his neck and tried to ignore the eye-watering miasma of cheap cologne. "Likewise, I'm sure."

"Can I inquire as to how your investigations are progressing? Do you have a suspect in mind?"

"Not as yet."

The light inside him smouldered like a bonfire of wet leaves in a flaking metal trash can.

"Well, that's too bad," he said. "You see, it's almost tourist season, and we don't want this awful business scaring off the few visitors we do get, now, do we?"

"Tourism's hardly my concern."

"Of course it isn't, of course it isn't." The mayor clasped his meaty hands together. "I am merely suggesting that the whole of Pontyrhudd might benefit from a swift resolution to this most regrettable of tragedies." The *r* sounds rolled like honey from his tongue.

"We're doing all we can," Holly assured him. "And I'm certain we can count on your full support?"

Davies smiled like a crocodile, revealing a gold tooth.

"Fair play." He looked her up and down with barely concealed speculation. "It goes without saying, Detective. If there's anything you need." He raised an eyebrow. "*Anything* at all, please feel at liberty to call me, whether it be day or night."

"Thank you." Holly inclined her head. "I'll bear that in mind."

Davies cupped her hand in his brawny palms and leered into her eyes. "Tidy. See that you do."

8.

AFTER THE MAYOR'S DEPARTURE, Holly decided she needed a walk. She needed to clear the smell of his aftershave from her nostrils, and she needed some time away from the hotel's musty rooms and corridors. And if she didn't burn off some irritation, she was worried she might end up smacking somebody in the mouth.

When Lao asked to tag along, she didn't object. Together, they stepped out of the hotel. Holly paused on the steps to turn up the collar of her coat and raise the hood of her hoodie. The rain still fell, visible only where it passed through the cone of light beneath each streetlamp. Across the road, sea and sky had merged into a single blackness, so that the orange-lit promenade resembled a walkway at the lip of the world, with nothing beyond but the lighthouse at the tip of the northern headland pulsing out its warning.

She turned left, and then left again, heading inland. Lao walked beside her in companionable silence. It was around eight o'clock. Few cars were around, and fewer people. Holly could see the blue light of television screens playing against the curtains of the houses she passed. With a killer on the loose, people were staying home. Even the pubs looked quiet—although that might have been due as much to the rain as anything else.

Following the main road, she kept walking until she'd left the town behind. In the night, it resembled the small, temporary encampment it had once been. Above it, fir trees whispered on the ridgeline. Small, furry creatures stirred in the bracken. Sheep muttered in their sleep. The air smelled of damp, rotten leaves, pine needles, short-cropped grass and sheep shit.

While the hills around Pontyrhudd had been tamed and coaxed into a patchwork quilt of fields and forestry, the damp valley floor remained in its natural state. It was a place of reeds and tufts, too boggy for farming, where the occasional scrap of dirty white sheep's wool waved from a barbwire curl, where an ancient dolmen stood sentinel on the banks of the shallow, rocky river, and low, clammy mists lingered, seemingly impervious to the breezes blowing in off the sea.

She had come out without a destination in mind, but her objective was inevitable.

Half a mile beyond the town's outermost cottage, a stile led to a path, which in turn led down to the wood-land flanking the river as it stretched towards the sea. Even now, fifteen years later and in total darkness, she could pick her way with confidence. She'd been here so many times. Although the last time she had been here, she'd almost died.

This was it: the clearing on the riverbank where her mother's body had been found, the muddy slope where, years later and wobbly on most of a bottle of strawberry wine, her teenage self had slipped and fallen into the water. Now she stood, breathless and listening, her senses heightened by the night. She could hear the river water running, the rain tapping through the leaves. And there, barely visible, the pale flank of the tree against which her mother's head had been resting when they found her. Its bark had long been peeled away, and initials were scratched into its hide. She ran her fingers over them, feeling the familiar, half-healed gashes. Somewhere here were her own initials, caryed on the night she'd almost drowned. Carved with an old penknife she'd lost when she fell, and which she'd have given almost anything to have in her hand again at that moment. Where were its rusty blades now? Enfolded in the silt at the bottom of the river, or already washed out to sea to cohabit with the bones of dead whales and murdered pirates? Water dripped on her from the overhead branches. An indifferent wind shushed its way through the canopy.

Eyes straining against the lack of light, she tried to imagine the scene as it might have been thirty-two years ago, when her mother lay sprawled on this patch of earth, her arms outstretched and her stomach gaping, her eyes pinned by twigs snapped from nearby branches. Holly pictured the steam rising from the exposed entrails, the vitreous humour seeping from the punctured sockets. But the horror of it was lost. She'd seen too many dead bodies in her career to be disturbed by the imagined details of a murder she was too young to remember.

Her most vivid recollection of this place was as the backdrop to her final night of normality. The night she'd come up here after celebrating her exam results and put her foot wrong on the edge of the river. After that night, everything had changed. She'd gone from reasonably normal student to haunted teen, confronted at every turn by the imperfections of humanity.

An owl hooted somewhere deep in the trees.

Lao said, "It must be weird to be back here."

Even in the dark, Holly could see the hearth light flickering inside the woman's skull.

"You have no idea."

She wished she'd thought to bring a bottle with her. She needed something to take the edge off. But maybe getting drunk in front of a journalist right now wouldn't be the wisest of career moves.

Instead, she said, "What do you make of the mayor?"

"Ieuan Davies?" Lao gave a snort. "He's full of shit."

Holly smiled in the dark. "I kind of got that impression. But is there anything about him I should know?"

"Like what?"

Holly leant against a tree. "Do you have any dirt on him?"

Lao laughed out loud. The sound was as bright as it was unexpected. "The man's been mayor of this town for more than thirty years. Of *course* I've got dirt on him." She flicked open an antique petrol lighter and the dancing flame illuminated her face. Holly watched her suck her cigarette to life and click the Zippo closed.

"What sort of dirt?"

Lao blew smoke at the overhanging branches. "What does your 'intuition' tell you?"

Holly shrugged. Her nose wrinkled at the bonfire scent of wet leaves and burning tobacco.

"I got the impression he was guilty of something, but it was all buried beneath a general patina of bastardy."

Lao laughed again. The end of her cigarette flared red as she inhaled.

"I don't have any proof." She looked around and leant in, lowering her voice. Smoke curled from her lips. "But I have a source who swears Davies was screwing the girl who got run over."

"Lisa Hughes?"

"She temped in his office up until last month, then she

left rather abruptly for the job at the hair salon."

"So Davies had a personal connection with her?"

Lao rocked back on her heels. "That's what I hear. And she wasn't the first, either. Word is the old letch has been knocking up temps and interns for decades."

The river babbled in the darkness. The Rhudd had been named for the reddish tinge of its water. Tradition had it the colour came from the blood of a wounded dragon. The more prosaic truth was that the hue prob-ably came from the sedimentary sand and mudstone through which the water passed. At least, that's what Holly had been taught in school. On a night like this, she could almost have believed the dragon story.

"I still don't get it," she said. "Even if Davies is our killer, and I'm not saying he is, why kill Daryl Allen in that particular way? Why not just hit him over the head with a rock or stab him through the heart instead of slic-ing him open and letting his guts fall out?" She rubbed at her forehead. "And why kill Owen the meat's boy the same way?"

A bat jinked through the clearing. The rain dripped and pattered into the undergrowth.

Lao sucked her teeth. "The only thing I can think is that he wanted to muddy the waters."

"By sticking skewers through a kid's eyes?" Holly shook her head. "I'm sorry, but it doesn't ring true. I can understand Daryl being killed. Lord knows the little shit seems to have deserved it. But that doesn't explain the mutilation, or the death of Mike Owen." She glanced around the clearing. Faintly, she could hear the intermittent hum of traffic on the main road at the top of the valley. "No, I have the feeling it's something way more sinister than that."

"But you're still going to check out Mayor Davies's alibi?"

Holly's lips twitched. She reached out, plucked the half-smoked cigarette from Lao's fingers, and took a deep, luxuriant drag. Held it in. Rolled it out. Flicked the butt into the river.

Said, "Hell, yeah."

9.

THE NEXT MORNING, when Holly came down for breakfast, Sylvia, the receptionist-cum-bartender-cum-waitress, showed her to a table by the window. Overnight, the rain had eased itself into nothingness, but the sky remained bruised and resentful. Holly ordered scrambled eggs and a pot of tea, and while she waited, watched a discarded crisp packet dance and jerk its way across the promenade.

A folded copy of *The Times* lay on the white tablecloth. The national news headlines were full of political jostling and foreign conflict. A couple of gruesome Welsh slayings rated little more than a six-line summary on page four. Not even a mention of the connection to her mother's death. If this had happened inside the golden halo of the M25, it would have been splashed all over the front pages.

When Sylvia brought over the tea, Holly put the paper aside and forced a smile.

"Thank you."

"You're welcome, Detective." Sylvia took off her half-moon specs and rubbed them on the hem of her apron.

Her glass eye stared up and to the right, making her look boss-eyed. She had dried egg on her sleeve and a chewed Biro behind her ear.

"Have you got anything to tell me today?"

"I beg your pardon?"

"The other night." Holly motioned a finger at the glass eye. "You told me what your eye had seen."

"My eye?" Sylvia's hand went to her cheek.

"You said it had seen secret things that happened in the woods."

The woman blanched. "I'm sure I don't know what you mean."

The light behind her eyes was a pale, attenuated thing. It flickered in ways Holly didn't understand. Instinctively, she drew back.

"I'm sorry," she said. "I meant no offence."

Sylvia pursed her lips. She flapped her hands as if searching for the right words. Eventually she muttered, "Enjoy your tea," and fled.

Holly watched the kitchen door flap in the poor woman's wake.

"Well," she muttered, "*that* went well."

She opened the pot, stirred the contents, and then poured herself a cup of amber sunshine.

Tea . . .

She knew it had a reprehensible history, as tied to the

shameful past of the British Empire as Volkswagen was to the Third Reich. But that hardly dented her enthusiasm for it. She was by all intents and measures an addict. Whatever else the day might bring, she couldn't function without her morning dose. That hit of fragrance and steam, followed by that first scalding, leathery sip. If an evening's worth of whiskey kept her from killing herself, it was the next morning's tea that truly kept her alive.

Her stomach grumbled. She could feel her metabolism rousing itself from its hibernation. But all she could think of was the case as it had presented itself to her: a deliberate hit-and-run, the driver mutilated and left in the town graveyard, and the butcher's boy pinned to his slab by steel skewers driven through his eyes. It all made as little sense now as it had last night. But if Lao was right about the mayor having an affair with Lisa Hughes, at least it gave her a place to start.

When Scott arrived, she asked him to run a complete background check on Ieuan Davies.

"I want to know everything," she said. "Prior convictions, known affairs, under-the-table payments. Everything."

"Yes, guv."

"And talk to Lao. She says she's got dirt on him. Find out what it is. He's a politician. If we're going to question him, I want to be holding all the cards before the game starts."

. . .

Davies wasn't too happy about being called down to the incident room to be interviewed. When he arrived, it was in the company of his solicitor, a birdlike old man by the name of Greaves.

Holly had cleared the room of all but herself and Scott. They took seats on one side of the main table and invited Davies and Greaves to sit on the other. A tape recorder sat in the middle.

"Before we start," Greaves intoned, intertwining skeletal fingers, "I would like to make it clear that my client is here of his own free will and has every intention of cooperating fully with your investigation."

Holly didn't smile. "I'd expect no less."

"And," Greaves continued, "we trust this conversation will be a mere formality, and that my client here will be under no suspicion whatsoever."

"Trust what you like." Holly looked at her watch and started the tape recorder.

"Interview with Ieuan Davies," she said, and gave the date, the time and the names of the persons present. Across the table, Davies struggled to contain his impatience.

"Is all this really necessary?"

"You tell us."

"What's that supposed to mean?"

"It means we have reliable information linking you to Lisa Hughes."

Davies glanced sideways at Greaves, who gave an almost imperceptible nod.

"My client is prepared to admit a relationship with the young woman in question but played no part in her death, or the subsequent murder of either of the young men concerned."

Holly fixed the old man with a glare. "Come on," she said. "You know the rules. You can't answer for your client. And if you persist in doing so, I can and will exclude you from these proceedings."

Greaves pursed his lips. His pencil-thin grey moustache twitched. He was quite evidently unused to being spoken to in such a manner. "I am well aware of the regulations, *Detective* Craig."

"Then try to fucking act like it."

Holly shrugged off her coat and let it fall across the back of her chair. Underneath, she wore a simple black T-shirt, which revealed the collection of bracelets crowding her left wrist and the list of names written on the inside of her right forearm. The names were those of the staff and children who'd died at Hawk Road Primary School. She'd written them on in Biro the day after the event and had been going over them with a pen every evening before bed, to keep them legible.

"Now," she said, "how about we stop flirting and cut to the chase? Mayor Davies, did you kill Daryl Allen or Mike Owen?"

Davies cleared his throat. "I did not."

"Where were you at the time of Daryl Allen's murder?"

Davies exchanged another glance with Greaves. "I was at home, asleep."

"And can anyone verify this?"

"Since my wife left, you mean?" Davies's cheeks flushed a deep and ugly red. "No, I was alone."

Holly saw the flicker behind his eyes and smiled. "You're lying."

"I beg your pardon?"

"You're lying. I can tell."

Davies opened and shut his mouth like a fish hauled out onto a wooden jetty. Beside him, Greaves looked fit to burst, but a warning glare from Holly was all it took to make the old man shrink back.

"Come on, Mr. Davies," she said. "We both know that's bullshit. Why don't you tell us where you really were?"

Ieuan Davies met her eye. He'd been the mayor here for decades; he wasn't used to people questioning him. His defiance was a fragile thing. All Holly had to do was stay silent until he couldn't stand it any longer.

"Okay," he said at last, his shoulders deflating, "I admit it. I wasn't alone the night Daryl Allen died."

Greaves tried to put a cautionary hand on his client's arm, but Davies shook him off.

Holly leant forward. "Who were you with?"

Davies took a deep breath and tipped his face to the ceiling. The overhead lights picked out the tears condensing in the corners of his eyes.

"Mike Owen."

"The second victim?"

"Yes."

"You were with him the night Daryl Allen died?"

"Yes."

Holly sat back in her chair. This wasn't at all what she'd expected, but she refused to let the surprise register on her face.

"In what capacity?"

Davies brought his eyes down to face hers. He looked haunted. "In a sexual capacity."

"So your alibi for the first murder is that you were too busy fucking the second victim?"

Davies winced. "That's . . . correct."

"And where were you when Owen was killed?"

"What time was it?"

Holly glanced at Scott, who checked his notes. "The pathologist estimates time of death for ten thirty," he said.

Davies slumped. "I was at a town council dinner until eleven."

"You have witnesses?"

"Only the entire council, and anyone else who might have been in the lounge of the Red Lion."

Holly pushed back in her chair and rose. "Thank you, Mr. Mayor," she said. "You've been very helpful."

She showed Davies and his solicitor to the front door. When she came back into the room, Scott was online, checking his emails.

"We have the initial forensic reports on Lisa Hughes and Daryl Allen," he said.

"Anything unusual?"

"They found some blue threads on Daryl's clothing."

"What kind of threads?"

Scott peered at the screen, reading. "The material most likely came from a police uniform."

"Who was first on the scene?"

"Perkins."

"Christ." Holly tipped forward on her toes until her forehead kissed the window's cool glass. Surely the constable would have known better than to contaminate a crime scene? "We're going to need to talk to him and find out if he touched the body."

"I'll give him a call." Scott picked up his phone but didn't dial. "Oh, and there's one more thing."

"What's that?"

"Lisa Hughes was six weeks pregnant."

Holly broke away from the window and read the email over his shoulder. "Now, *that* is interesting," she said. "Lao told me Lisa was working for Davies until a month ago."

"Do you think it could have been his child?"

"That might explain why she argued with Daryl. It might even explain why Daryl killed her, and why Davies killed him. But once again, it doesn't explain why Mike Owen's dead."

"Doesn't it?" Scott sat upright in his chair. "Perhaps Owen found out what Davies had done. They were sleeping together, after all. There could have been clues. Bloodstains, maybe. Whatever. Perhaps Owen found out and threatened to expose Davies, and Davies decided to shut him up?"

Holly tapped a fingernail against her upper teeth. "That certainly sounds plausible."

"Should we call the mayor back?"

"No." She shrugged. "While I don't deny it might be fun to drag him back here and try to browbeat a confession out of him, the fact remains that we don't have a single shred of physical evidence linking him to any of the murders."

"So what do we do?"

Holly made a face. Overhead, she could hear the pipes wheeze and clank as one of the hotel's guests had the audacity to try and run a bath in the middle of the day.

"Our jobs," she said.

10.

LATER THAT AFTERNOON, HOLLY'S superiors summoned her back to headquarters in Carmarthen to brief them on the state of the investigation. High-profile cases tended to make or break careers. With the media now starting to involve themselves, everybody in the chain of command was busy covering his or her arse. It was the same political, primate hierarchy bullshit that had almost torpedoed her career after the slayings at Hawk Road School. Everybody wanted credit for success, but nobody wanted to take responsibility when things went tits-up. If she hadn't transferred back here before the knives came out, she had no doubt she would have been one of the officers scapegoated for the Met's botched handling of the incident.

As it was, she didn't mind the drive. The sun was out. The hills and hedgerows were green. The verges were yellow with daffodils. And it was good to get out of Pontyrhudd for a few hours. As soon as she hit the main road, her chest felt less constricted.

She followed the A487 south, passing farm tracks, old

brick barns with corrugated iron roofs and the occasional lay-by. From time to time she caught glimpses of the sea to her right. During her years in London, she had forgotten how effortlessly and breathtakingly beautiful the Welsh countryside could be.

The signs and road markings were all in English and Welsh. The terraced houses and shops lining the main street in Aberaeron had been painted pink, yellow, red, blue and green. Downshifting for the long climb out of the town, she passed a caravan park advertising vacancies, and then fields replaced the sea views as the road swung south, away from the coastline, and she changed onto the A486 and then the A465, winding her way down through the countryside to Carmarthen and the brick buildings of the HQ.

. . .

The meeting went pretty much as she'd expected it to. First they praised the work she'd done so far, then they expressed disappointment at the lack of immediate arrests, and finally the whole thing wrapped up with a series of veiled threats and a stern admonition to find closure as soon as humanly possible.

The only person to express any kind of sympathy was her immediate line manager, Detective Superintendent

Rajkumari Srivastava. After staying silent during Holly's briefing, preferring to listen and take notes, she approached her in the corridor afterwards.

"How are the people I sent you?" Srivastava was ten years older than Holly. Veins of silver ran through her dark hair.

Holly leant back against the wall with her hands in the pockets of her coat. "So far, with the exception of Scott, they've been a useless shower of bastards."

"That doesn't sound like a very fair assessment."

"It's the only one I've got."

"And what you said in there about having a suspect but no evidence?"

"All true, I'm afraid."

"No cards up your sleeve?"

"Not this time."

Srivastava grimaced. "That's a shame."

"Sorry."

The two women stood in silence. Finally, Srivastava said, "Do you think he's going to kill again?"

"Davies?" Holly shrugged. "I've no idea."

"If you get even the slightest inkling, I want you to bring him in." Srivastava leant forward and lowered her voice to an urgent whisper. "I don't want any more bodies, not with the media breathing down our necks."

Holly twisted her lip. "We got six lines in *The Times*."

The other woman was not amused. "And if there's an-other murder, it will be twelve lines," she growled. "And they'll all say one thing. Can you guess what that will be?"

"That it's our fault?"

"No." Srivastava shook her head. "They'll say it's *your* fault. Yours personally. I'll make sure of it."

• • •

Holly wandered back to her car feeling as if someone had sucked all the air out of her chest. She was starting to think she might have been better off staying in London to face the music. At least then she could have stayed in her comfortable, book-strewn upstairs flat in Finsbury Park. She wouldn't have had to leave her cats with friends while she searched for a place within commuting distance of Carmarthen. And she certainly wouldn't have had to deal with the emotional fallout of returning to Pontyrhudd. She leant against the car and watched the sun dip low in the afternoon sky. Of all the places she could have ended up, what had pos-sessed her to apply for transfer back to this end of Wales? She could just as easily have gone to Yorkshire or Scotland. Hell, she could have quit policing alto-gether and become a fucking waitress. Why on earth had she thought coming back here would be a good idea?

. . .

By the time Holly reached the turning for Pontyrhudd, dusk had stolen across the fields and hedgerows. The lights were on in the Galleon, but the valley behind it lay in darkness. She turned left, onto the road that led down to the town. As she did so, a pickup truck pulled off the pub's forecourt and began to follow. She saw its lights in her rearview mirror but thought nothing more of it. Most of the Galleon's regulars came from Pontyrhudd or the surrounding farms, so it was hardly a surprise to see one heading down the valley from the Galleon. And besides, with Srivastava's words still ringing in her ears, Holly had enough on her mind.

It wasn't until the truck's lights filled the interior of her car that she frowned. It had come right up to her rear bumper.

"What the fucking hell are you playing at?"

If the driver was local, he must know they were approaching a sharp bend. This was no place for him to try overtaking. She blipped her brakes twice, hoping to make him back off a bit. And, to her relief, the headlamps shrank in her mirror. For a moment, she was tempted to call Scott. He could get a patrol car to meet them at the end of the road, and then she could arrange for the twerp to be breathalysed as he pulled into town. There had already been one drink-related death on this road in the past few days; perhaps she should make an example of this idiot?

Ahead, the road veered right, hugging the valley's contours. Black-and-white chevrons pointed the way. Holly downshifted from fifth to fourth, and then fourth to third. She was still concentrating on lining up for the turn when she was thrown forward against her seat belt as the truck rammed into her back end. The hire car slithered, and she saw the crash barrier approaching. Beyond it, all she could see was darkness. She hit the brake, but the truck was pushing too hard. Her left wing mirror splintered against a warning sign. Tyres squealed. Her car shook and rattled around her. The lights in her mirrors dazzled her. In desperation, she wrenched the wheel to the right. The car slewed around, but not far enough. They were moving too quickly. Her left wing crumpled and tore against the crash barrier. Glass exploded around her, and then everything tipped sideways as her car burst through into empty space.

During her time as a uniformed police officer, Holly had seen enough road traffic accidents to know that in a rolling car, the driver's head and neck were the most vulnerable to catastrophic damage. A head whipping to the side could snap vertebrae and sever a spinal cord. So in the second of sickening free fall available to her, she tucked her chin into her chest and wrapped her arms around her head. It was all she could do.

11.

WHEN THE CAR FINALLY lurched to rest, Holly found herself upside down in her seat, hanging from her belt. She thought she'd probably blacked out at some point but wasn't sure. Everything had happened so rapidly. Through the shattered windscreen, she could see gorse and bracken. Thankfully, her car's headlights were still working; otherwise she'd be in total darkness.

"Fuck."

She reached up and pressed the seat belt release. The lock clicked and she fell onto the inside of the car's up-turned roof. Shards of glass rained around her, and the whole wreck groaned.

Rather than bouncing and rolling all the way to the floor of the valley, it seemed her car had caught itself in a tangle of undergrowth. But now it was rocking and she wasn't sure how securely it was held. One ill-judged move might dislodge the vehicle from its prickly cushion and send it and her cartwheeling to the bottom of the cwm. She held her breath until the creaking stopped. Then, moving as gingerly as she could, she scrambled through the broken side window.

As she moved, her left leg flared with pain, and she feared her knee might be broken. Glass fragments cut her hands. Gorse needles scratched her face. Her nostrils were full of the twin scents of freshly disturbed earth and leaking petrol. Thirty feet above, she could see the distended remains of the crash barrier against the night sky. Using her gloved hands and good leg, she hauled herself away from the car. If that petrol caught, she wanted to be far enough from it to escape the resulting blaze. Luckily, with the weather having been so shitty for the past few days, most of the vegetation had become sodden with rainwater and unlikely to catch unless subjected to the most extreme heat.

"I should have stayed in London," she muttered, wiping away tears and gritting her teeth against the pain in her leg. "You can't fall off a fucking mountain in London."

A mile or so farther along the valley, she caught a glimpse of taillights winding their way down to Pontyrhudd. But all she could think about right now was getting clear of the wreck.

And then, quite suddenly, the hairs prickled on the back of her neck, and she knew she wasn't alone. A cloaked, cross-legged figure seemed to be sitting at the edge of her peripheral vision. But when she turned her head, all she could see were clumps of limp bracken.

Nesting crows nagged and grumbled in the trees. A ragged cape swished against the skyline. A laugh so faint, Holly couldn't swear she'd actually heard it. And then, as abruptly as it had arrived, whatever it was that had been on the grass beside her had gone. She couldn't feel it any more. The grass was just grass, the bushes just bushes. And her leg was an ingot of molten agony. She dug in her coat pocket for her phone. Despite a starred screen, it still worked.

Scott answered on the third ring.

· · ·

"Who was that?" Jen sat up in bed and rubbed her eyes.

"The new guvnor." Scott swung his legs out from beneath the blankets. "She's been in an accident."

He dialed 999 and ordered an ambulance, then looked around for some clothes.

Through eyes narrowed against the bedroom light, Jen watched him pull on a pair of jogging bottoms and a hooded sweatshirt from his gym bag. She had been with him for four years now, and they had been married for one; she had become used to late-night phone calls. She understood they were a part of his job, but that didn't mean a small part of her didn't resent each and every time the phone rang and he disappeared into the night. She hated being left alone in the sheets, not knowing when he would be back, or what he might see while he was away.

"What's she like?"

"The guv?" Scott opened his sock drawer and pulled out the first pair on which he laid his hand. "She's all right, I suppose. A bit severe, maybe. Dresses like a tramp."

"Short skirts and that?"

Scott laughed. "Not that kind of tramp."

Jen watched him grab his keys from the nightstand and a jacket from the back of the chair.

"Be careful," she said.

"Always am." He leant down and kissed her. "Don't wait up."

She grinned and stretched like a cat. "Never do."

"*Nos da, cariad.*"

"*Nos da.*"

. . .

The ambulance took Holly to the nearest A&E department, which was up at Bronglais in Aberystwyth.

"Hello, love," the consultant said when he finally arrived in her cubicle. "Do you speak English?"

Holly nodded.

"What's your name?" He had a friendly smile, curly

hair and a strong jaw speckled with dark stubble.

"DCI Craig."

"Well, DCI Craig." He made a note on his clipboard. "Let's take a look at you, shall we? Are you hurt?"

"My knee."

With difficulty, she removed her ripped and muddy jeans, and he examined her leg.

"Anywhere else?"

Holly held up her wrist. "I cut myself on some glass."

The consultant leaned in close. He smelled warm, as if he'd just climbed out of bed. He cleaned and dressed the wound and then shone a penlight in her eyes.

By the time her leg had been X-rayed, it was almost four in the morning. The good news was her knee wasn't broken. The bad news was the ligament behind it had taken some punishment. Somehow, she'd caught her foot behind the clutch pedal and her whole leg had wrenched sideways during her car's cartwheel down the hillside. The consultant strapped her leg and prescribed her some painkillers, but she was still going to have to spend the next three or four weeks on a crutch.

"And you've had a bit of a nasty shock," he said. "I want you to try to take it easy for the next few days. Lots of rest."

Holly gave a snort. "Fat chance of that," she said.

. . .

Scott drove her back to Pontyrhudd. The sky had started to lighten as they passed the site of her crash. Police tape festooned the broken barrier.

"You were bloody lucky," Scott said.

Holly didn't reply. Her bloodstream was full of codeine and paracetamol, and she was thinking of the presence she'd sensed beside her in the darkness. The presence every rational fibre of her being told her had been nothing more than a trauma-induced delusion.

. . .

Scott dropped her back at the hotel.

"Do you need any help on the stairs?" he asked.

Holly opened the car door and used the crutch to lever herself into a standing position. It hurt like hell. The sea breeze tousled her auburn hair. The sun would be up in an hour, and the gulls were starting to stir.

"No," she said.

Scott blinked as if slapped. "I'm only trying to be helpful."

His soul glistened like a polished stone at the bottom of a sunlit rock pool. Holly looked down at him and bit back the reply she had been about to make.

"I'm sorry," she said, relenting. "I don't mean to snap at you. None of this is your fault, and you have been very helpful already."

Scott stuck his bottom lip out, which made him look like a pouting schoolboy. "Okay."

"I mean it. Thank you for driving me back." She forced a smile. "It's just it's going to take me some time to get used to this stick, and so I may as well start now."

Scott glanced at her crutch. He looked somewhat mollified. "Right then," he said. "If you're sure?"

"Of course I am." She jerked her thumb in a get-out-of-here gesture. "Now get back to your wife before she reports you missing."

Scott grinned. "See you tomorrow, guv."

Holly pushed the door shut and watched as he drove away. When his car finally disappeared around the bend at the end of the promenade, she turned and awkwardly hauled herself up the hotel's front steps.

Behind her, a pale moon had just set over the water, and the breeze carried the salt stench of the incoming tide.

12.

HOLLY FOUND IT DIFFICULT to get comfortable in bed. She couldn't find a position in which her knee didn't hurt, and the morning light shone through the curtains, making the room too bright. It was only the painkillers and the fact she'd been up all night that allowed her to eventually fall into fitful, agitated sleep.

She dreamed of close-packed trees and river water babbling over black rocks, and woke around eleven and stared up at the hotel's painted ceiling.

Somebody in this town wants me dead, she thought. Running her off the road like that hadn't been a warning. It had only been sheer luck the car hadn't rolled all the way to the bottom of the valley. No, whoever had been behind the wheel of that truck had meant to kill her and make it look like an accident. And the only person she could think of who might want her dead was the person who'd murdered Daryl Allen and Mike Owen.

Which might mean I'm getting close, she thought. And the only person she had so far interviewed as a suspect was Ieuan Davies.

Had the mayor really tried to have her bumped off? She hadn't been impressed with him when they first met, but the only way to be sure was to have another conversation with the man.

She rolled out of bed and pulled on a fresh pair of jeans.

First things first.

Leaning on her crutch with one hand and gripping the banister with the other, she hobbled downstairs in search of tea.

. . .

If Sylvia was curious about Holly's injuries, she didn't show it. She simply brought out a pot of tea and a rack of toast and placed them on the white linen tablecloth.

"Nice morning," she said, peering through the dining room window at the whitecaps out on the bay.

"Mm-hmm." Holly had never been great at small talk. She poured herself a cup of tea and added a dash of milk.

"Yes," Sylvia continued. "It's a nice morning, but I think we're going to have a bit of rain soon enough."

"Oh, have you seen the forecast?"

Sylvia looked surprised. "Oh, good heavens, no. I never listen to the *wireless.*" She whispered the last word as if referring to something scandalous and immoral.

"I've got to be honest with you: I can feel it in my eye."

"Your eye?"

"The false one." She tapped the side of her head. "It itches when there's bad weather coming."

"Really?"

"You mark my words." The young woman wiped her hands on her apron. "It'll be raining old ladies and walking sticks by three o'clock, just you wait and see."

Something out on the promenade snared her attention and a beatific smile stole onto her face. "Dew," she said. "Will you look at that?"

Holly followed her gaze and beheld Mrs. Phillips tottering barefoot in the direction of the hotel. The old woman's pink feather boa writhed out behind her in the wind. She had one hand to her head, holding a silver tiara in place, and the other at her side, clutching her high heels.

"Out *carousing* all night." Sylvia's tone dripped disapprobation. "Traipsing back here at this hour. Doing the walk of shame, I'll be bound. And now she'll be wanting one of my fry-ups, you'll see."

She turned and bustled off into the kitchen, still muttering.

Moments later, Mrs. Phillips stuck her tousled head around the dining room door and trilled, "Good morning, Detective!"

"Good morning, Mrs. Phillips."

"I heard you had a bit of an accident last night."

"Where did you hear that?"

Mrs. Phillips gave an airy wave. "Oh, you know what this place is like, love. If you lose your virginity at lunchtime, someone will have found it and brought it home to your mam in time for tea." She glanced at the crutch leaning against the back of Holly's chair. "But you're all right, though, are you?"

"Just bruises and a torn ligament."

"Thank heavens for that. There's been enough death and misery in this town of late." And with that, she straightened her tiara, crossed the room like a galleon in full sail and barged her way into the kitchen.

"Sylvia!" she called. "Get that bloody bacon on. My stomach thinks my throat's been cut."

. . .

Scott arrived just as Holly was finishing her tea. With his hair gelled back and his jaw freshly shaven, and dressed in a light grey suit with a blue shirt and yellow tie, he looked annoyingly perky for someone who'd spent most of the night in a hospital waiting room. You'd never know he'd missed out on a good night's sleep.

"*Bore da,* guv. How are you feeling?"

"I'll survive." She watched him hover uncertainly, shifting his weight from one polished shoe to the other. "What have you got to tell me?"

Scott looked sheepish. "It's about Mr. Davies."

Holly pushed her cup and saucer away from her and reached for her crutch. "If you're about to suggest we bring him in for further questioning, I quite agree."

Down by the water's edge, an old man was in the process of setting up a fishing rod and deck chair. On the promenade, a pair of seagulls bickered over the carcass of a dead pigeon.

"That's the thing." Scott rubbed the back of his neck. "I think we can rule him out as a suspect."

"How so?"

"The man's been murdered."

13.

THE MAYOR'S HOUSE WAS situated at the top of a steep lane and overlooked the town. From the front, you could see the sea. From the rear, fields and woodland and, in the distance, the outbuildings of the abandoned RAF base a couple of miles up the coast.

His body lay stretched across the kitchen table. One arm dangled loosely. A shoe lay on its side. As with the previous two victims, his eyes had been punctured—this time with pencils—and an incision made in his abdomen.

Holly let her weight rest on her crutch.

"Who found him?"

"The cleaner," Scott said. "Her name's Mrs. Andrews. She comes in twice a week to give the place the once-over. She found him when she turned up for work at nine this morning."

Holly's eyes roved over the kitchen's counters. A dirty plate lay in the sink, and a single mug sat next to the kettle, waiting to be filled.

"So you've had people here since nine?"

"Jensen and Potts secured the scene, and the forensic people have already been in. We just thought we should let you see the room before we moved the body." A private black-liveried ambulance waited outside to transport the corpse to the coroner's mortuary. Its driver stood out on the pavement, smoking a cigarette.

"Is Potts the one that was being an asshole at the butcher's shop?"

"That's him."

"Why didn't you call me earlier?"

"To be honest, we figured you could use the rest."

Holly decided to ignore that. "This cleaner," she said. "She has her own key?"

"And an alibi for last night. She was at the bingo until eleven."

"And what was the time of death?"

Scott checked his notes. "As far as the doc can tell from a preliminary examination, somewhere between six and nine thirty. But I'm hoping to narrow that down once the pathologist takes a look at him. And the coroner's going to want to take a look and all."

Holly frowned. "So Davies might already have been dead by the time I got run off the road?"

"It's possible."

"Damn." Holly massaged her forehead with the fingers and thumb of her free hand. She glanced back to the solitary dirty plate in the sink.

"Where's Mrs. Davies?"

"Staying with friends in Cardiff, apparently."

"Has she been informed?"

"An officer went round this morning to break the news."

"How did she take it?"

Scott rubbed his jaw. "She wasn't that upset by all accounts."

"Do you think she might be a suspect?" If Lao's gossip was to be believed, the woman's husband *had* slept with Hughes and Owen. Could all this be the work of a jealous, neglected spouse?

"I'll ask the Cardiff people to look into her whereabouts last night."

"Okay, and get the uniforms to canvass the neighbours, to see if any of them noticed anything out of the ordinary."

"Will do."

"And I want a full debriefing from Jensen and Potts."

"Yes, guv."

• • •

Scott drove Holly back to the hotel, where, waving away all offers of help, she hobbled her way from the kerb to the incident room and collapsed into one of the chairs surrounding the central conference table. The rest of the staff were all out knocking on doors and looking for witnesses, and the room had the air of a recently vacated wedding reception, when all the guests have gone and the band have packed and left, leaving only hastily scribbled notes, half-eaten sandwiches, and the vague smell of Lynx deodorant.

She threw her crutch onto the table and turned up the collar of her RAF coat.

"Damn," she said.

She had been certain Davies was the killer. But with him out of the picture, she had no one else. And she knew Srivastava would be breathing down her neck, pushing for a swift resolution. Now the town's *mayor* had been whacked, the national papers were really going to start paying attention. Pontyrhudd was about to turn into a media circus, and all Holly wanted to do was crawl into bed with a bottle of bourbon strong enough to strip the enamel from her teeth.

Scott went over to the kettle and made two cups of tea. He placed one in front of her, along with four sachets of sugar.

"Thank you," she said. He really had been quietly and unobtrusively helpful over the past twenty-four hours—sitting with her in A&E, taking care of the paperwork when all she could focus on was the pain in her knee, and then driving her back here at first light. And his soul was clear and untarnished as sunlight dappling through spring leaves. Where had all the guys like that been when she'd been in her early twenties? She gave him the once-over from the side of her eye. If she'd been a few years younger, she might have considered falling for him. But she was in her early thirties now; he was too young for her, and he was married. And besides, she was his boss. It had been a hell of a long time since she'd found anyone worthy of her trust, but trying to initiate any sort of relationship with this young man would be a mistake of epic proportions. All it would achieve would be to blemish the one thing that really attracted her to him—and after that, it would lose all point. No, she'd take his loyalty and she'd accept his friendship, but love was something to whose absence she'd long ago resigned herself. She just hoped his wife appreciated what she had. So often, youth was entirely wasted on the young. By the time you were old enough to know what to do with it, it had already slipped through your fingers.

"So." Scott nodded towards the whiteboard on the wall, where all the hand-drawn arrows pointed to a photo of Davies. "What's the plan now?"

Holly stretched out her bad leg and grimaced.

"Unless the uniforms turn up a witness, we're back to square one."

"I was afraid you were going to say that."

"Is this case that important to you?"

Scott laughed.

"Are you kidding?" He pushed back his hair with one hand. "Of course it is. I mean, not only there's a killer loose in my hometown, I also get to work with an SIO with your reputation." He spread his hands. "I don't want to sound mercenary, but if we crack this, it could make my career."

"Right now, that's a big 'if.'"

"Yeah." He flicked a crumpled Post-it Note across the table. Upstairs, pipes groaned and clanked.

Surely, Holly thought, after the night she'd had, no one would blame her if she just went and pulled a blanket over her head? She stifled a yawn. She'd been in a serious car crash, for heaven's sake; she needed time to gather her wits and recover.

But, a snide little voice whispered in her head, *wouldn't that just suit Srivastava down to the ground? Take to your bed and admit you're not up to this, and she'll kick you off this case—and probably back into uniform—without a second's hesitation.*

If Holly wanted to be the one to solve this case, she'd have to find a way to soldier on. And now that she thought about it, she really *did* want to solve it. The mystery had its hooks in her, because she was starting to accept that in order to unravel it, she'd also have to disentangle the circumstances of her mother's death. Something that had started as a hit-and-run uncomfortably near her old stamping grounds had now taken on the aspect of a deeply personal crusade. She was the senior investigating officer on this case, and she wasn't about to let injury, exhaustion or Srivastava prevent her from seeing it through. To do that, she was going to need allies. And, she realised, the only people in Pontyrhudd she really trusted were Scott and Lao.

She should probably make an effort to start being nicer to them.

She glanced at the clock.

"Give Amy Lao a call," she said. "It's nearly two o'clock. Let me buy you both some lunch."

. . .

They ate in one of the few surviving cafés on the front. The mirrored walls made it look wider than it was. In the booths, black electrical tape had been used to patch the vinyl seat covers. Holly ordered fish and chips and a pot of tea from the laminated menu. Lao asked for a bacon sandwich with black coffee, and Scott opted for scrambled eggs on wholemeal toast.

Today, Lao wore olive cargo pants and a plaid work

shirt. She had apparently spent the morning working on an obituary for Ieuan Davies.

"I can't believe he's dead," she said through a mouthful of sandwich. "Don't get me wrong, he was a corrupt bastard. But nothing ever seemed to stick to him. I thought he'd be around forever."

Scott picked at his eggs, which were overdone and sweating grease. "And Davies was our only suspect," he said.

Lao looked to Holly. "Is that right?"

Holly hadn't touched her food at all. Perhaps it was a side effect of the codeine, but after one look at the soggy batter and limp chips, her stomach had decided it really wasn't that hungry. She sat wrapped in her big coat with her injured leg out as straight as she could get it.

"I'm afraid so."

"Damn." Lao swallowed and put the rest of her food aside. "I was hoping you'd invited me here to give me a scoop on the identity of the murderer."

"Unfortunately not." Holly took a sip of her tea. It wasn't a patch on the tea at the hotel, but it was warm and wet, and better than no tea at all. "I guess you could say we're currently 'between suspects.'"

"But somebody tried to kill you last night?"

Holly rubbed her thigh. "Yeah."

"No leads from that?"

"Only that it was a black or dark grey pickup truck."

Lao made a face. "Half the farmers around here drive trucks like that. Did you get a look at the driver?"

"It was dark. I didn't see much more than headlights, to be honest."

"And you've made no progress with your mother's murder?"

Holly shook her head and her red hair danced. "It was thirty years ago. I wouldn't know where to start."

The reporter pulled a cigarette from behind her ear and tapped it on the cracked Formica tabletop. "I might be able to help you with that." She leaned forward on her elbows. "The guy who was at the paper before me, the original journalist who covered your mother's story, still lives here in Pontyrhudd. He's a bit of an eccentric, but I'm sure he'd be happy to talk to you about it."

14.

FOLLOWING LAO'S DIRECTIONS, SCOTT drove the
three of them up to the old RAF base. Holly hadn't been
there since she was young, when her grandfather still
worked as a mechanic. Although in those days the base
had been winding down, planes had still come and gone;
Jeeps had still patrolled the site, chasing flocks of seabirds
from the runways; and in the summer, the yellow
Sikorsky rescue helicopter occasionally battered overhead, on its way to retrieve tourists who'd ventured out of
their depths at Aberystwyth or Fishguard.

Now most of the buildings had been demolished, and
only a couple of the hangars remained; dandelions
pushed their way through cracks in the tarmac, and a
herd of Jersey cows grazed between the taxiways, their
udders rosy and swollen.

"There." Lao pointed to the far corner of the base,
where a small caravan nestled up against the perimeter
fence.

Holly peered dubiously through the fogged-up windscreen and twitching wipers. The caravan looked like

something from a postapocalyptic society. A wind turbine clattered on its roof. Tin cans jangled on strings. A threadbare armchair sat under a tattered awning, and chickens fussed in the long grass.

"That's where he lives?"

"I told you, he's an eccentric."

The car bumped across the pasture to the caravan. As it pulled up outside, the caravan's door opened and a bearded old man emerged. He wore a frayed deerstalker and mirrored sunglasses and cradled a shotgun in the crook of his arm.

"That's him?" Holly asked, pushing back in her seat.

"Oh yeah, that's him all right." Lao squeezed Holly's shoulder. "And don't worry, he hardly ever loads that thing."

Lao opened the door and stepped out, shading her eyes from the drizzle.

"All right, our Steve?" she said.

The man gave a solemn nod. His beard was the speckled colour of a badger's ass, and his voice had deep reverberation. "Hello there, Amy. And who's this you've brought to see me, now?"

"This is the inspector leading up the murder investigation," she said. She beckoned Holly to get out of the car. "DCI Craig, this is Stephen Woodrow."

"Good morning, sir." Holly eyed the gun. "I understand you might be able to help us."

"Help you, is it?" The man looked amused. He propped the shotgun against the side of the caravan and removed his glasses. "Well, I guess you'd better come in, then."

• • •

Scott and Lao waited outside as Holly followed the old man through the door. Inside, the caravan looked more like a ransacked study than any sort of habitable abode. Books and papers had been stacked on every flat surface. Dog-eared photos and yellowing articles had been pinned to the walls. Sagging piles of newspapers fanned across the floor, and the air smelled of mildew and pipe tobacco.

Holly guessed Woodrow to be somewhere in his early seventies. Deep creases fanned from the corners of his eyes, and when he removed the deerstalker, the top of his head was as bald and mottled as the surface of the moon.

A dim light, like the worn glow of an elderly paraffin lamp, shone in the depths of his skull.

Holly said, "I believe you covered the murder of Alice Craig."

He squinted at her from beneath untamed brows. "You're her daughter, aren't you?"

"Yes."

"I heard you'd run away to London."

"Well, I'm back now."

"And you're with the police?"

"We're investigating a series of killings in Pontyrhudd. We think there might be a connection to my mother's death."

Woodrow reached up to scratch his beard. "It wouldn't surprise me. A lot of dark stuff went on back then. Especially up here."

"At the airbase?"

"Mm-hmm." The old man pulled out a pipe and began filling it.

"What kind of stuff?"

"Experiments." He tamped down the oily strands of tobacco with his thumb, clamped the pipe stem in his teeth, and pulled a lighter from the pocket of his tweed jacket.

"What sort of experiments?"

Woodrow puffed out his ruddy cheeks. "You wouldn't believe me if I told you. You'd think I was a daft old fool, same as the rest of them."

Holly glanced at the blurry photos taped to the walls and windows. Black smudges against grey skies. Long-range shots of hangars and other buildings.

"My mother was killed down in the valley."

Woodrow applied the lighter flame to the brown fibers sticking from the pipe's bowl. He sucked and huffed the thing into life, producing clouds of smoke as he did so, and then pocketed the lighter.

"Yes," he said. "I remember. I covered the case."

"Amy Lao seems to think you had an idea who the killer might have been."

"Does she now?"

"Do you?"

Woodrow champed at the pipe. He puffed smoke at the ceiling. "You might have got your green eyes and your red hair from your mother," he said, "but your father was one of the airmen stationed here."

"What?"

"Yeah, I'm pretty sure."

"But my father—"

"He died a couple of years after your mam, didn't he?"

"Yes."

"He knew the truth."

Holly shoved a couple of paperbacks from the arm of a sofa and perched on the edge of it, taking the weight from her bad leg. She wasn't sure what to say. Half a dozen responses battled for utterance. Finally, she settled on asking, "Are you sure?"

"Sure as I can be."

"That's . . . a lot to take onboard."

Woodrow sucked his pipe. He scratched the backside of his threadbare trousers. "Of course," he said, "I might be wrong. I *was* taking a *lot* of acid back then."

. . .

Holly stepped back out into the drizzle. Lao and Scott were hunched beneath the caravan's red-and-white striped awning while chickens gossiped around their feet.

"Are you all right, guv?"

"Yeah."

"Any luck with identifying the killer?"

"Not so much."

"Well, what did he say?"

Holly shook her flame-coloured hair. "He's a fucking space cadet. Sorry, Lao, no offence intended."

The journalist shrugged. "None taken. I know he's not always as lucid as he could be."

Scott took out his car keys and turned up his collar. "Where now?"

Holly looked out across the deserted aerodrome, remembering it as it had been back in the days when her grandfather was still alive and she still had a normal childhood, before her accident cursed her with the ability to peer behind a person's eyes. "Home, I guess."

"Back to the hotel?"

"Back to the drawing board."

They were opening the car doors when a Land Rover came bouncing towards them from the direction of the hangars. A florid-cheeked man leant his head from the window.

"What are you lot doing by here? This is private property!" His eyes came to rest on Lao. "You're the woman from the local paper, aren't you? What's occurring?"

Holly stepped up to the vehicle. "My name's Detective Chief Inspector Craig. We came here to interview Mr. Woodrow."

"That old nutter? What's he gone and done now?"

"He hasn't done anything. We thought he might be able to help us with our enquiries."

"And did he?"

"Not so much."

The man drummed his fingers on the Land Rover's hard plastic steering wheel. "Well then. I don't mean any disrespect, but you can pack up and bugger off. Like I said, this is private land."

He watched them until their car turned onto the public road, and then he turned his Land Rover and drove back in the direction of the hangars.

"Who was that?" Holly asked.

"That's Rees Thomas," Scott said. "He's a local builder.

His firm built my mam's extension."

"He moved into property development a few years ago," Lao said from the backseat. "He and Mayor Davies were pretty tight, by all accounts. That's how he got planning permission to turn the airfield into a holiday village."

Holly frowned. "A holiday village?"

"You know, caravans and chalets, a swimming pool, all that jazz."

15.

IN A SIGNIFICANT AMOUNT of pain, and with no leads to go on, Holly decided to take a break. Leaning awkwardly on her crutch, she struggled her way uphill through the rain to the old terraced street where her grandfather had lived. Here, she found the house in which she'd spent most of her childhood and teenage years. She hadn't been back to it since the day she packed her case and left for London. Now, seeing it sandwiched between its neighbours, she couldn't help thinking it looked smaller than she remembered.

Like the houses on either side, it had walls of grey stone and redbrick edging around its doors and windows. Unlike the houses on either side, it was empty, and had lain so since the death of her grandfather. In accordance with his wishes, Holly had received the keys and deeds in the mail. But she'd never felt the urge to come back here and clear the place. As far as she knew, it remained exactly as it had been left on the day he died.

Having been unsure what else to do with the house key when it arrived in an envelope from her grandfather's solicitor, she'd simply clipped it onto the ring with the rest of her keys. Now she pulled the bunch from her pocket and opened the door.

The lock turned just the way she remembered.

She pushed the door open against a pile of accumulated papers and flyers. Damp air swirled into the stillness of the hallway, shivering the dry, brittle leaves of the dead spider plant on the windowsill at the bottom of the stairs, and she stifled the urge to call out a hello. This felt like a stranger's house, and she felt very much like a trespasser. Without removing her coat, she hobbled through to the kitchen, which was just as her grandfather left it that morning. Used teabags lay piled in a saucer beside the kettle, a dirty frying pan lingered on the stove and a moldy dishcloth hung over one of the taps. A well-thumbed mystery novel sat on the dining table, next to a copy of the *Racing Post*. The clock ticked on the wall. The place had the flat, stale odour of a house that had been closed up and unoccupied for weeks, but it felt too late in the evening to be opening windows. Instead, she hobbled over to the cupboard where he used to keep the booze and helped herself to a bottle of supermarket own-brand whiskey. The glasses were in the next cupboard, but she was too tired to try pouring with one hand, so she eased herself down onto one of the dining chairs and took a drink straight from the bottle.

A pack of her grandfather's cigarettes lay on the table. Without thinking about it, she drew one and lit it using the plastic lighter beside the pack. The tobacco was as stale as sawdust, but when the smoke hit her chest, it made her light-headed the way she remembered. The last of the rain dripped from her fringe and ran down her face, and her stomach closed up on itself like a fist. And suddenly she was crying, heaving out great wracking, smoky sobs.

She cried for her grandfather, and for the girl she had once been; for the dead bodies with their punctured eyes, and the mother she had never really known; for the pain in her leg and the fact someone had tried to kill her; and finally, she cried for the dead children at Hawk Road School.

When the tears ran out, she sat for a while with her head in her hands, letting her hair hang over her face.

God, I must look a state, she thought, wiping her eyes on her cuff. *Not that there's anyone here to see.*

She pulled her damp coat tight around her shoulders, fighting back a sudden craving for physical comfort. She couldn't remember the last time she'd been hugged, or the last time someone had lain beside her and held her all night while she slept. Right there and then, she would have given almost anything for the chance to doze off enfolded in another's arms.

Unable to bear the emptiness and silence upstairs, she slept on the sofa with the TV for company, dozing fitfully in front of its flickering light until six a.m., when her grandfather's cat—which must until now have been dependent on the kindness of neighbours—came in through the cat flap and woke her by pawing gently at her cheek and demanding to be stroked.

. . .

As the sky lightened, Holly sat by the front window with the cat on her lap and the curtains open and watched the clouds over the sea turn from mackerel grey to salmon pink. She heard the first bus of the day crunch its gears as it wheezed its way up the valley towards the main road. A few houses away, a dog barked.

She glowered at the slate rooftops of Pontyrhudd, not knowing which of them hid the killer she sought. Three people had fallen victim since the death of Lisa Hughes, and Holly herself had almost been the fourth. What was so important about Hughes that her demise had sparked such a trail of violence? And what, aside from the way the bodies had been mutilated, did any of it have to do with the murder of Alice Craig?

Hughes had been pregnant at the time of her death—either by her boyfriend or by the mayor. But both of them were dead now. Was the pregnancy the key to the riddle, or just an unfortunate coincidence? And then there was Owen, the butcher's boy who'd been having an affair with Ieuan Davies. If this were a vendetta against Davies, Owen's murder would be understandable—but in that case, why kill Daryl Allen? If anything, the kid had been wronged by Davies. Killing him served no purpose. Unless killing him somehow avenged Lisa Hughes. But then why kill Mike Owen?

The questions kept circling around in her head, snapping at one another's heels. Whiskey fumes throbbed behind her eyes. The cat squirmed beneath her touch, its little animal soul glowing like a brazier.

Her grandfather had adopted the creature after she left for London, and now she couldn't remember its name.

"I guess I'll have to call you Fred," she said, scratching the cat behind its ears. In return, Fred nuzzled her hand. He didn't care what he was called; he just wanted a *cwtch*.

As Pontyrhudd woke and shook itself, ready for another day, Holly found her thoughts drawn back to the night of her accident.

She had been eighteen years old, celebrating her A level results with a group of friends from school. There had been twelve of them altogether. They'd built a fire in the woods and sat around it drinking strawberry wine and telling ghost stories. There were the usual tales of escaped maniacs and young couples terrorized by ghostly figures with hooks for hands. But then, as the night wore on and the wine went to their heads, one of the boys started telling the story of Ragged Alice.

"It was on this very spot," he said, before going on to relate the grisly fate that had befallen Holly's mother. The story had become part of the mythic history of Pontyrhudd. Everyone had heard it, and doubtlessly a few even believed it.

The kid telling the story poked the fire with a stick, sending up sparks.

"To this day," he said, "Ragged Alice wanders these woods with twigs in her eyes, blindly taking her vengeance on anyone foolhardy enough to venture in here alone. Especially—" His eyes lit on Holly and his face froze.

"Oh shit," he said, looking pale as realisation dawned.

Holly clenched her fists. Everyone in the circle was looking at her. She felt her cheeks flush at the onslaught of their embarrassment and pity.

"Shut up, Brendan," she said. She scrambled to her feet. She just wanted to hide.

"Holly, I'm sorry. I didn't think."

"Oh, fuck off."

She turned and blundered out of the firelight, not caring where she was going, wanting simply to get away before she burst into tears. Brambles scratched her fore-arms. Branches raked her hair. Someone called after her, but she didn't stop to see who it was.

Why did it have to be my *mother?* Why did she have to be the one they tiptoed around? Even now, on the night her classmates celebrated their future, she still felt snared by the talons of the past.

She came to the edge of the River Rhudd and stopped. The rust-coloured water bubbled and sang in the shadow of the trees. How easy it would be, she thought, to throw herself in and be borne away by the current.

Behind her, her friends' voices were asking her to come back, not to be silly. She ignored them. She was going to that London in a few weeks. She had her university place confirmed. The only way to break the chokehold of the past was to go there and never look back. To purpose-fully lose touch with everyone who currently knew her and never set foot in this godforsaken valley again.

In London, she could start with a clean slate. She could build a new life, somewhere nobody knew her. No longer would she have to be the girl whose mother had died; freed of that restraint, she could simply be Holly Craig—and Holly Craig could be whoever the hell she wanted to be.

A fat, buttery moon had risen over the trees. Its light danced on the river, and Holly smiled. She had made her decision. In a few weeks' time, she would be gone. She would leave all this behind, and Pontyrhudd would slowly forget she'd ever existed. All her friendships would be over. The only person with whom she would stay in contact would be her grandfather, and even then only via a monthly letter.

The night air smelled of mossy soil and warm bracken. It prickled against her skin. It was the arse-end of August and her arms were bare and open to the night. The stars she could see through the leaves overhead were hard, brittle little points of light that seemed to map the way to a new, happier tomorrow.

"Make the most of me while I'm still here," she told the flitting bats and softly whispering trees. "Because I'm never coming back."

Jet engines whined at the airbase. A shadow moved in the corner of her eye, and a voice spoke words she couldn't interpret. She turned her head to follow the sound, but as she did so, she felt the riverbank give way beneath her heel. She cried out, but the impact of the water cut her short. The coldness stole her breath, and the current tumbled her over and over, until she couldn't tell which way was up. Her fingers scrabbled for purchase. The water roared in her ears.

This is it, she thought, fighting the urge to gag. *I'm going to drown.*

The muck tasted rank and salty in her throat, like the water from an unclean fish tank. She gagged again, stomach muscles convulsing as her diaphragm went into spasm. Even though her eyes were shut, she could see sparks.

Why was this happening?

Weighed down by her sodden clothes, her legs felt as if they were pushing through treacle. The need to breathe was turning her inside out, and she knew she couldn't hold on. She knew she was going to die.

Just not yet.

She clamped her jaw so hard she feared her teeth would splinter.

Not yet . . .

Her body tried to retch. Her limbs thrashed. Every pulse thumped like a drumbeat. And then, just as she was on the verge of giving up—of surrendering herself to the dreadful, choking darkness—her head hit a submerged rock, smacking her into unconsciousness and forever changing her life.

She would have drowned had her friends not managed to pull her from the water and administer CPR until the ambulance crew arrived. As it was, the paramedics reckoned she'd spent ten minutes clinically dead, with no pulse or respiration. Even thinking about it now made the back of her neck prickle.

. . .

At first, Holly had sought a rational explanation for her newly acquired gift. She had read somewhere that sharks were able to sense the bioelectrical auras surrounding prey animals in seawater, and home in on them when the water became too dark or murky for sight alone to suffice. Marine biologists referred to this ability as "electroreception." Could that explain her ability to see inside a person's head? Was she simply visualising electrical impulses?

On further investigation, she discovered that over millions of years, sharks had evolved special receptors that allowed them to sense other creatures—receptors the human body simply didn't possess. Trawling the lower half of the internet, she came across claims by psychics and healers who said they were able to perceive multicoloured auras surrounding people, but as far as Holly could tell, their stories lacked a single shred of rigorous scientific proof.

Proof was important to her. Even as a teenager, she possessed the kind of calm, analytical mind and thirst for understanding that would later help her excel as a detective. She had the same intuition and gut instincts as anyone else, she just felt unable to completely believe them until she had found solid, reliable evidence. She prized science and common sense above all else. So what scared her about the paranormal wasn't the possibility that it might exist; it was the knowledge that confirmation of its existence might upend everything she held dear.

Unable to find any other explanation, she soldiered on regardless. She saw psychiatrists and counselors, but no combination of therapy or medicine had been able to alleviate her condition. The only cures she had found were exhaustion and strong whiskey. So she worked hard and drank harder. And somehow, she staggered along from one day to the next. And slowly she learned to read the mottling she perceived around the lights in some people's heads and correlate it to guilt for past deeds. Every person's inner light burned at a different temperature. Some were as soft and steady as the glow of a paraffin lamp; others hard and bright as an exploding star. Those who felt bad about their transgressions carried their regret as stains on their soul. And gradually, Holly found she could interpret those smudges to the point where she sometimes knew when to press for a confession and when to release a suspect as innocent. She could often tell if a suspect had committed a crime simply by the accumulated stains smothering their internal radiance. She just didn't like to think about the metaphysical implications of what she saw. As far as she was concerned, she merely had a talent for picking up on a person's shame and remorse.

And if she used the word soul to describe the light behind a person's eyes, it was simply because she couldn't think of a better shorthand.

$$\cdots$$

Holly's leg hurt too much to negotiate the steep hill that led down into the town, so she phoned Scott and he came to collect her.

"I brought tea," he said, handing her a polystyrene cup from one of the new cafés on the high street.

"Oh my God, thank you." She'd tried to make herself a cup earlier, but the milk in her grandfather's fridge had been a couple of years past its sell-by date.

Scott smiled at her reaction. He drove her down to the hotel, where she took up position on a chair in front of the whiteboard in the incident room.

Nothing on the board had changed since yesterday. The arrows still pointed to Davies as the most likely suspect.

"We've got the fingerprint comparison from the knife that killed Mike Owen," Scott said, checking his laptop.

"And?"

"It wasn't Davies."

Holly pried the plastic lid from her tea. "Who was it?"

"We don't know."

She blew the steam from the tea and took a cautious sip. "Maybe Davies had an accomplice."

"And that accomplice then turned on him?"

"It's a possibility."

Scott rubbed his chin. "You could be onto something there, guv."

"It's a stab in the dark, but let's see if we can put together a list of Davies's associates. Anybody he might have hired to do his dirty work."

"I'll get Potts and Jensen onto it."

"And call Amy Lao. I get the feeling she knows which of Pontyrhudd's closets hold the most skeletons."

Scott's mobile rang, and Holly waited while he took the call. When he had finished, he said, "I've got some bad news, guv."

Holly sighed. "Okay, let me have it."

Scott rubbed the tip of his nose. He shifted his weight from one foot to the other. "Autopsy results show Davies was killed half an hour after you were being run off the road."

Holly felt a hollow space open in her stomach. "Are you sure?"

"I'm afraid so. If the person who rammed you was waiting in the Galleon car park, the chances are they'd been waiting there for some time. They couldn't have known exactly when you were going to return. They must have gone straight back to Davies' house."

"So if we'd have been later, Davies might still be alive?"

"Yes, guv."

Holly put a hand to her leg. Her knee hurt and her calf muscles kept cramping with the effort of keeping her foot raised. "This just keeps getting better and better."

Scott walked over to the whiteboard. He picked up a green pen and drew a question mark, circled it, and stepped back.

"Our new suspect," he said. "The invisible bloody man."

16.

LOW TIDE WAS THE only time it was possible to cross the causeway joining the northern headland to the lighthouse. As Amy Lao followed Mrs. Phillips towards the white tower, she could smell the black seaweed drying on the cobblestones. Crabs scuttled out of their way. The sea lapped at the edges of the footway.

Mrs. Phillips had once been the lighthouse keeper's sister, but her brother had retired when the installation had been converted to full automation, and had since died. Where once an operator had been needed to light the lamp each evening, now the whole thing ran with little more than a quarterly technician's visit. Nevertheless, old Mrs. Phillips still came out here once a month to tend the window boxes on the empty, whitewashed cottage at the foot of the tower.

The old woman had dressed for the job at hand, putting aside her habitual finery for a thick cardigan, a pair of baggy dungarees and a stout pair of Wellington boots. She had put up her hair and fastened it in place with a pair of knitting needles—an affectation that struck

Lao as inappropriate given the recent murders and caused her to lightheartedly speculate whether Mrs. Phillips had been the killer all along and now intended those needles for the eyes of her next victim. Lao smiled to herself as she tried to picture the ninety-year-old overpowering the butcher's hulking son.

She pulled out a cigarette and lit it, sheltering the lighter flame with her free hand. Gulls jostled one another on the edge of the causeway. Wings flapped and beaks snapped.

"Come along," Mrs. Phillips called over her shoulder. "We haven't long." Once they made it across, they'd have two hours to complete their business before the turning tide re-covered the causeway. Lao hoped that would be enough. She'd agreed to accompany Mrs. Phillips this morning because she wanted to test a theory, however unlikely it might seem now she was actually here.

At the end of the causeway, they climbed sea-slicked steps to the cottage, which was a single-storey stone building with thick walls and high windows designed to withstand spring tides and winter storms. From here, Lao could see no signs of forced entry, but she still tensed as Mrs. Phillips produced a key from her dungarees and unlocked the front door.

Let's see if I'm right . . .

The heavy wooden door opened on salt-rusted hinges.

Fresh air curled into the cottage's only downstairs room, disturbing the curtains and white lace hem of the table- cloth. It blew dust from the picture rail and Lao felt herself relax. Nobody had been here in some time, and probably not since Mrs. Phillips's last visit.

The cottage consisted of a sitting room and hearth, a small bedroom, a scullery and a cramped bathroom. All were empty and showed no signs of having been dis- turbed. But in order to completely disprove her theory, Lao knew she'd have to check the tower as well. Although each building had its own separate entrance, they also shared a connecting door that would have allowed the keeper to access the tower even in the worst of weathers. This door wasn't locked, and led into the base of the lighthouse proper.

Lao found herself in a circular room. Oilskins and sou'westers dangled from hooks like the dried remains of flayed sea creatures. Coils of rope mouldered quietly in a wooden crate. A bucket of old shells sat beside the door- mat. With a little curse, Lao crossed to the bottom of the spiral staircase and began to climb.

Tiny windows had been sunk through the tower's heavy walls so that every ten steps gifted her a blurred, pockmarked view of either the sea or the town. Was she looking out on the Atlantic Ocean or the Irish Sea? In the four years since she'd moved from Birmingham to Pontyrhudd, she'd never been entirely sure where the boundary lay. Having been schooled in Hong Kong, British geography had never been one of her strengths. She made a mental note to look up the answer when she got back to the office.

She passed through the first storey, which had been done out as an office. Shipping charts covered the walls. A large, old-fashioned radio sat on the desk with its chunky knobs and dials. A larger window faced out into the bay, and a pair of dusty binoculars lay on the sill.

Nothing out of the ordinary.

She continued upwards but paused when Mrs. Phillips called up the stairs.

"Are you up there, Amy, *bach*?"

"Yes, Mrs. P."

"Well, what are you doing up there?" The old woman started climbing. Lao could hear her huffing and wheezing with the effort.

"I'm just taking a look around."

"Well, why didn't you say so?" The old woman appeared around the curve of the stairs. Her cheeks were flushed. "I could have given you the tour."

Lao smiled. She'd liked Mrs. Phillips ever since first meeting her three years ago, when she'd covered the local amateur dramatic society's production of Noël Coward's *Blithe Spirit*. Mrs. P had delivered a rousing and largely improvised performance as Madame Arcati that wandered off script so frequently the other actors were left floundering in her wake.

"I'm nearly done. Only one floor left."

"Then give me a second to catch my breath, and we'll go up together. I'd like to show you the view."

. . .

From the room that housed the lamp, Lao could see the centre of Pontyrhudd nestled in the mouth of the valley and its terraced residential streets stacked up against the hillsides. With a palpable air of pride, Mrs. Phillips pointed out the local landmarks: the chapel on the headland, the control tower of the airbase, the bingo hall, and the new supermarket that had opened on the outskirts of town. Lao nodded dutifully at each of them, while simultaneously looking around for evidence of occupation. But she could see no footprints in the dust, no discarded food wrappers or items of clothing to suggest anyone had been using this place as a bolthole.

"Are you all right, *bach*?" Mrs. Phillips looked concerned.

Lao shook herself. "I'm sorry, what were you saying?"

"I was just pointing out the mayor's house by there. But you looked about a million miles away for a second there."

"I was just thinking."

"That this would make a great hideout for our mysterious murderer?"

Lao blinked in surprise. "How did you know?"

"Because I know the way you think. The tide cuts this place off from the mainland for twenty hours a day, and nobody really comes here, save me; and I only come once a month."

"Why didn't you say anything?"

Mrs. Phillips's eyes crinkled. "I knew we'd be all right, love. This is the lighthouse. Nothing bad happens here."

"How can you be so sure?"

"My brother wouldn't let any harm come to us. He's good like that."

"Your brother?"

"Alan, the lighthouse keeper."

"Isn't he, you know . . . dead?"

"Of course he is. But that doesn't stop him keeping an eye on the place. It was his life, see?"

Lao turned her attention to the waters of the bay. She didn't know how to respond. Her grandmother often spoke of ghosts and spirits, but it had been a long time since Lao had subscribed to such beliefs.

Beside her, Mrs. Phillips turned to look up at the great glass lantern occupying most of the available space.

"The light keeps the town safe," she said.

Lao didn't look around. She'd been hoping to find a

lead here. If she'd broken this case, or at least uncovered the clues that led DCI Craig to catch the culprit, it could have been her ticket out of here and into a proper news-room in Birmingham or London. She might even have been able to write a book off the back of it. That was why she'd invested time in a theory that was, in the cold light of day, ridiculous, and why she now found herself stand-ing here listening to an old lady talk about ghosts.

"I thought the light was there to warn ships," she said, not bothering to keep the disappointment from her voice.

Mrs. Phillips sucked her yellow teeth. "Let me tell you a story." She leant against the window, still looking up at the light.

"During the war," she began, "the RAF used the air-field up there for training Hurricane pilots. They used to ship them here from all over the country to teach them how to fight. Anyway, one night they were practicing fly-ing in the dark, and one of the pilots got into trouble. He tried to get back to the runway, but he was losing height, so he jumped out. His plane only just cleared the top of this tower and crashed into the dirt just the other side of the chapel."

"Did he survive?"

Mrs. Phillips pursed her lips and shook her head. "No, love. I'm not going to lie to you. He was too low for his parachute to open, see? They found his body the next morning, floating in the water just near these rocks."

"That's horrible."

"The whole town was very sad." She held up a gnarled and crooked finger. "But the thing is, they still say that if you stand here when there's no moon and it's properly dark, you can sometimes hear that Hurricane pass over the tower, still trying to get home.

"Because you see, *bach,* this light isn't here to keep ships away." Mrs. Phillips brushed her painted fingernails against the smooth face of the gigantic lens. "It's here to guide all the poor lost souls stranded out there in the dark."

17.

AT LUNCHTIME, SYLVIA BROUGHT a plate of ham sandwiches to the incident room. As the rest of the team dug in, she drew Holly aside.

"I've seen something," she said, polishing her half-moon spectacles on the hem of her apron. "I don't know if it will be helpful or not."

Holly tried to concentrate on the young woman's good eye, rather than the false one. "What is it?"

"I was up by the mayor's house night before last, and I saw someone coming out of the property."

"What time was this?"

"About half midnight. I'd just been up to me mam's house to tuck her in and walk her dog around the block."

"Who did you see?"

Sylvia looked both ways and lowered her voice. "I don't want to get anybody into trouble, mind."

"Don't worry about that. Just tell me who you saw."

"It was one of your lot, in uniform."

Holly leant in close. "One of the constables?" Nobody had mentioned any visits to her. "Did you see which one?"

"It was Neil Perkins. I recognised him but didn't think anything of it. But then, when I heard poor Mr. Davies had been murdered, it struck me as funny, you know?"

"Perkins? You're sure?"

"Of course I'm sure. Mam was at school with his dad. I'd know him anywhere."

"Okay, thanks."

Sylvia carried her empty tray back to the kitchen. Holly beckoned to Scott, and they stepped out into the corridor.

"We've got a witness who saw Perkins coming out of Davies's house at half twelve yesterday night."

"You're kidding?"

"No, I'm deadly fucking serious."

"Who was it?"

Holly shifted on her crutch, trying to get her knee comfortable. "Sylvia from the kitchen."

"And you believe her?"

"She'd rather die than drop anybody in the shit." Holly glanced at her watch. "Where is Perkins, anyway?"

"I'm not sure. I'll put in a call."

"Tell him to come straight here. At the very least, I think he owes us an explanation." Holly let her shoulder rest against the wall, taking some of her weight. "And when you've done that, run his fingerprints against those we got from the butcher's shop."

Scott raised his eyebrows. "Do you really think he might be a suspect?"

"Remember the blue fibres they found on Daryl Allen? Forensics said they might have come from a police uniform."

"But when I asked him, Perkins said he tried to revive the boy." Scott rubbed his ear. He frowned. "Couldn't they have gotten onto the body that way?"

Holly shook her head. "Who tries to revive a body with its guts hanging out and twigs driven through its eyes?"

"Fair point. I guess I hadn't thought of it like that."

"Neither had I until just now." Holly took a breath, considering her next move. She'd have to be careful. She couldn't accuse a fellow officer of murder on the basis of circumstantial evidence and speculation.

"Okay," she said. "Our first priority is to find Perkins and bring him in for questioning. Until then, I don't want you to say anything to any of the others. We keep this between ourselves until we're sure."

"Understood. Leave it to me, guv." Scott straightened his tie. "I'll ring him now."

. . .

While Scott made his call, Holly hobbled outside and

sat on the bench that leant against the hotel's front wall. It felt good to be off her feet. She propped the crutch against the armrest and pulled her grandfather's pack of cigarettes from her coat pocket. She hadn't smoked at all in London. But now she was back in Pontyrhudd, it seemed old habits were resurfacing.

Next thing you know, I'll be wearing too much eyeliner, hanging around the arcades, and mooning over My Chemical Romance.

The wind chopped spray from the swell. Sunlight came down in slants. She lit up and blew a line of grey smoke at the sea and clouds. She had forgotten her hometown could be so pretty. She'd spent so much time trying to distance herself from the painful memories of her adolescence, she'd neglected to keep hold of the ones that really mattered—the way the rolling surf glittered white in the low-slung midday sunlight; the personified, angry hunger of the gulls; and the way the fresh green bracken shoots clustered on the hillsides above the town like the camouflage of a sleeping army.

Was this how Dorothy had felt when she'd woken up to find herself back in Kansas?

Holly took another drag on the stale cigarette and imagined she could feel the smoke scouring every square nook and cranny of her endless, fractally branching lungs. But, to be honest, she doubted it was any more harmful than the toxic crud she'd inhaled every day on the streets of Holloway and Finsbury Park. It was, she decided, the voluntary nature of the act that made it feel so debauched. Instead of battling her way through London's traffic fumes and industrial pollution, she was sitting out here in the crisp spring air, wantonly dragging pollutants into the delicate membranes of her chest. When Scott joined her, he wrinkled his nose at the smell.

"Perkins isn't answering his radio or his phone," he said.

"That's not a good sign."

"This might be a misunderstanding."

"And it might not. But the only way we'll know for sure is if we talk to him."

"I've got the other constables out searching. I haven't told them why we need him, but if he's still in Pontyrhudd, they'll find him."

"And what do we do until then?"

Scott slipped his hands into his pockets and smiled. "Well, it's lunchtime. I thought maybe you'd let me buy you a drink."

Holly took a final drag on her cigarette and flicked the stub into the gutter.

"Now that," she said, "is the first sensible thing I've heard all day."

. . .

The Red Dragon sat at the far end of the promenade. It was a traditional Welsh pub. You could tell by the linoleum floors and scuffed barstools and the jar of pickled eggs beside the cash register. The clientele were mostly old soaks, with rounded shoulders and souls smouldering with the same sepia hue as their nicotine-sallow complexions.

Scott went up to the counter and came back a couple of minutes later with a half pint of bitter for himself and a double Jack Daniel's for her.

"Thank you."

"You're welcome." They took a table by the window. "How's the leg?"

"Hurts like fuck. Did you get hold of Lao?"

"She wasn't answering her mobile. I left a message."

Holly watched Scott as he sipped his beer like an old maid sipping tea. His light burned clear and bright, like that of a child. No great regrets burdened his soul. No sunspots of guilt to dim his inner fire. She'd never met anyone so apparently guileless. The fumes from her own drink reawakened the dormant leftovers of the whiskey she'd consumed the previous evening, triggering a queasy, seasick sensation behind her eyes. She could see he was waiting for her to speak, but she wasn't sure what she was supposed to say. Around the bar, the low mutter of conversations returned. The dog went back to sleep. The clock over the optics struck one thirty.

Holly sipped her Jack Daniel's. She really wanted to get drunk. It was the only way she knew to shift a whiskey hangover, and the only sure way to damp down her peculiar gift enough to be able to ignore the shadows in the heads of those around her. Only her commitment to finding the killer kept her from draining the glass in a single swallow.

After a few minutes of companionable silence, Scott cleared his throat. "Have you thought what you'll do when this is over?"

"The case?"

"Are you going to stay in Pontyrhudd, like, or are you off back to Carmarthen?"

"I honestly hadn't given it any thought."

"Must be strange to be home, though?"

Holly shrugged. "I haven't thought of this place as home in a very long time."

"You've got your granddad's house here, mind."

"Yes." She swirled her glass around, watching the amber liquid slosh like oil. She knew Scott was just being friendly, but his interest in her plans made her uncomfortable. Having been self-reliant and solitary for so long, she wasn't used to sharing her private life with others.

"I might sell up," she said. "I really haven't decided."

Scott sipped his beer. "Well, for what it's worth," he said, "you've got to be the most interesting DCI we've had around these parts in a fair while."

Holly smiled despite herself. "Now that," she said, "I can believe."

Behind her, the pub door opened, letting in a shaft of daylight. Dust motes danced in and out of the sudden illumination. Fresh air swirled around her ankles.

"Don't look now," Scott said, "but here comes Woodrow."

Holly turned to see the old kook framed against the sky as he waited for his eyes to adjust to the gloom of the bar.

"Is DCI Craig by here?" he boomed. He had his deerstalker firmly jammed in place, and his beard looked like a windblown thicket.

Oh God, Holly thought. *What fresh hell is this?*

"I'm here," she said, raising a hand. Stephen Woodrow turned his chin towards the sound of her voice.

"Ah, yes." He strode over, seemingly unaware of the number of eyes watching him as his hiking boots knocked on the wooden floor. "I have something for you." He dropped a plain brown A4-sized envelope onto the table. "I don't know if it will be of any help, but I thought you'd better see it."

Holly picked up the envelope from the table and opened the flap. Inside she found a black-and-white photograph.

"What is it?" Scott asked.

"I'm not sure." She placed the photo on the table where they could both see it. The picture had been taken at night and showed the old Neolithic stones that stood where the twists of the River Rhudd formed a kind of promontory on the valley floor, surrounded on three sides by the rust-coloured water. Portable lamps illuminated the stones. Electrical wires had been strung between them. Various scientific instruments lay on the grass. To one side, a couple of white-coated technicians bent over a box covered in dials and valves. Both wore plastic safety goggles, and one of them was smoking a pipe. To the side, a pair of armed RAF officers stood guard. One was her grandfather. She didn't know who the other one was, but there was something familiar about his eyes and the shape of his chin.

"That's just down the hill from where Lisa Hughes died," Scott said.

"It's also about a hundred yards from where my mother was killed."

"What are they doing?"

"Beats me."

Woodrow leant forward and tapped the picture. His

breath stank of vodka, pipe tobacco and onions. "There's a time stamp at the bottom," he said.

Holly's throat went dry. "Holy crap."

"What is it?" Scott looked concerned.

"This was taken about ten minutes before my mother was killed. She was out there in the woods that night, just yards away from whatever was going on here."

"Do you think there's a connection?"

"There has to be."

Holly looked up at Woodrow. During their first meeting, the man had said something about experiments at the old base. But what kind of experiment was this? What were they measuring? Holly knew granite was radioactive. If the stones were made of granite, had the technicians in the picture been trying to measure the radiation coming off them? Perhaps they were trying to establish the age of the monument. But if that was all they were doing, why had they felt it necessary to have an armed guard accompany them? And why do it at night? And what possible connection could this have to her mother's death? Holly's grandfather would never have stood by while harm came to Alice. She remembered him as an uncompromising, fiercely moral man. He'd never have permitted anyone to commit such an act of cruelty and disfigurement on his daughter.

"There's one more thing," Woodrow said. He slid a

second photograph from the envelope. This one showed a concrete bunker with the trefoil symbol for radiation stencilled on the door in black paint.

"What's this?"

"The old fallout shelters up at the base. They were for the use of the base personnel in the event of a nuclear attack."

Holly frowned at the picture. She recognised the position of the hangars in the background, which meant the photo had been taken from roughly the place where Woodrow's caravan now stood.

"They're not there now?"

Woodrow scratched his beard. "No, that's the thing. When the base was decommissioned, they moved a lot of stuff down into the shelters and then backfilled the stairwells with concrete. They even bulldozed the aboveground entrance, to make it harder to find."

Scott looked puzzled. "Why would they do that?"

The old man frowned at him and then laid the pictures side by side on the sticky pub table. His blackened fingernail touched the photograph of the stone circle. "My guess is they made contact with something."

"Contact?"

"They found something at the circle. And whatever it was, they didn't like it."

"So." Scott had the look of a man struggling to see

the relevance of what he was being told. "What happened?"

Woodrow's hand moved to the image of the old, now-demolished bunker. "They entombed it beneath several tonnes of concrete."

"So whatever it was, they didn't want anybody to find it?"

Woodrow leant forward and lowered his voice. "Or maybe they didn't want it getting out."

He sat back and crossed his arms, letting the words hang between them. Holly and Scott looked at each other.

Scott's phone rang.

"It's Jensen," he said. "They've found Perkins's car."

· · ·

Scott pulled up behind the abandoned police car and helped Holly from her seat. Detective Constable Potts and a couple of uniforms were already present. When Potts saw her climb from the car, he turned away with a roll of his eyes.

"Any idea how long it's been here?" she asked.

Potts turned back to her with an insincere smile and rapped his knuckles against the bonnet. "He left the headlights on."

"Did you turn them off?"

"No, the battery's flat."

"So the car might have been here for anywhere between three and six hours?"

"Seems that way. He left the door open, too." Potts tucked the front of his shirt into his straining belt. He was being condescending, as if all her questions were those of a slow child. "At least, it was open when we got here."

They were standing among the sand dunes to the south of town. Tough grass shivered in the wind. Holly cast around. "Any footprints?"

"If there were, the wind's covered them."

"Or he intentionally covered his tracks."

Potts scratched his cheek dubiously. "I suppose. Not very likely, though, is it? Silly sod probably just wandered off."

Leaning heavily on her crutch, Holly glowered at him. "Can I remind you we're in the middle of a murder investigation? Until we know for certain what we're dealing with here, I think it would be best to consider *all* eventualities. Don't you agree, *Constable*?"

The fat man sighed. "Yes, guv."

"Now, I want this whole place treated as a crime scene. Wherever Constable Perkins is, I want him found."

Potts rolled his eyes again. "Yes, guv."

Not trusting herself to respond and worried she just

might go ahead and punch the supercilious prick, Holly turned and instead hobbled through the dunes to the beach at the foot of the southern headland. The sea wind scoured some of the fumes from her head. A gull mewled. She couldn't blame Potts for not taking things seriously. Pontyrhudd had never seen a spate of killings like this. The poor man was out of his depth and in denial. Being dismissive was just his way of protecting himself. Nevertheless, his attitude rankled. He reminded her too keenly of some of the Neanderthals she'd had to work with on the Met—old-school detectives who'd resented her rapid ascent through the ranks.

Her leg hurt like hell. She dug a couple of ibuprofen from her pocket and swallowed them dry.

That was the thing about death, though. It affected different people in different ways, and you could never really predict how anyone was going to react to a mangled corpse. In her time, she'd seen strapping six-foot coppers go weak at the knees while attending their first RTA. Others fell apart afterwards, when all the mess had been cleaned away and their minds started chewing over the horrors they'd seen. You'd have to be made of stone not to let that part of the job get to you. Sometimes flippancy and an obstinate lack of imagination formed a shield against such trauma. The less you allowed yourself to care, the fewer times you got hurt.

Thinking about it in those terms, she could understand Potts's boorish behaviour, but his apparent distain for her as a female officer didn't make it any easier to deal with.

The names of the dead at Hawk Road scrolled through her mind. She didn't fight them. Instead, she lowered herself onto a sandy tuft and pulled out a cigarette.

We've all been hurt, she thought. *But there's no need to be an arsehole about it.*

She savoured the heat of the smoke in her mouth.

Steps led from the beach to the top of the headland, where the village primary school looked across the town to the chapel on the other promontory. It was a redbrick Victorian building with high, arched windows and a concrete yard enclosed by a tall wire fence. Holly remembered it well. She had attended the school from the age of four to the age of ten, at which point she'd transferred, along with the rest of her class, to secondary school in Aberystwyth.

The lane from the town to the school was a single track with tall hedges. She recalled the exertion of walking up it on frost-rimed mornings, when the frigid air scoured her lungs and everybody had red cheeks and wore scarves and mittens knitted for them by their nans.

What had happened to all those little girls and boys?

As a ten-year-old, she'd loved her friends. As an only

child, they were her brothers and sisters, and she'd thought they'd be together forever. They'd had so many plans and dreams. But now, like dreams, they had evaporated from her life, scattered to the winds by the passing years. Doubtless a few still lived in the town, but she wasn't sure she'd even recognise them if she passed them in the street. And even if she did, it wouldn't matter; the children they'd once been would be gone, leaving only grown-up strangers in their place.

For a moment, all she could think about was the devastation at Hawk Road. The flashing lights. The TV cameras. The dead being stretchered out of the classrooms, one by one.

Then something clicked in her head, and she recalled what Sylvia had said when asked if she was sure she recognised Neil Perkins.

Of course. Mam was at school with his dad.

Could it be that simple? Lisa Hughes, Daryl Allen, and the butcher's boy had all been the same age as Perkins—and in a town like this, that could only mean they'd all been in the same year at school. For the first time, that gave her a definite connection between the first three victims and the missing constable.

She called for Scott and, when he appeared from between the dunes, explained her reasoning to him. Scott looked out to sea and rubbed the back of his neck.

"It might be a coincidence," he said.

Holly felt a flush of irritation. "It might," she snapped, "but right now, it's the only connection we have. So let's go back to the hotel and try and work out what it means."

18.

AFTER RETURNING FROM HER sojourn to the lighthouse with the nice young Chinese girl, Mrs. Phillips retired to her room in the Royal Hotel. The exertion had worn her ragged, and she needed forty winks in order to gird her loins for whatever the evening might bring.

She'd been living in room number six for close to a decade now. Feather boas hung from the coat hook on the back of the door. Lipsticks and pots of powder covered the dresser, and glittering gowns packed the wardrobe. The air smelled of lavender and cheap perfume. She kicked off her shoes and sat on her unmade, squeaky bed. The view from the flaking sash window showed curtains of rain drawing in from the sea, just as Sylvia had predicted.

A half-empty bottle of peppermint schnapps stood on the nightstand. Mrs. Phillips poured a generous measure into her ceramic tooth mug and gulped it down in a single swallow.

She could see the ghosts in her peripheral vision. As usual, they lingered like afterimages in the corners of the room. Thin, translucent beings it was easier to ignore than acknowledge. Some would have messages they wanted her to pass on for them—usually heartbreakingly mundane reminders to cancel the milk or walk the dog—while others seemed unaware of anything around them, simply huddling close to their fellows as if trying to draw warmth from their companionship.

Mrs. Phillips had been seeing them since she was a girl. They held no fear for her. If anything, she felt pity for them. Poor things. They didn't know why they were still here or what they were supposed to do. So they occupied the spaces in the corners of her world, haunting run-down hotels, out-of-season penny arcades, and the broken stalls in public restrooms. They clustered behind bus stops and in the doorways of boarded-up shops, loitered in the pale glow of takeaways, wringing their hands and muttering to themselves.

"And you lot can shut up," she told them. She didn't have a lot of time for complainers.

That was one of the nice things about her brother: he never grumbled. He was quite content pottering around the lighthouse, champing on the end of his pipe and keeping a weather eye out for the first signs of fog rolling in off the Atlantic. He never seemed to listen to her, but occasionally he'd look up and give her a smile. In that respect, being in a room with him now was exactly the same as it had been when he was alive.

"Silly old sod."

She replaced the mug on the nightstand and levered her stocking-clad feet up onto the bed.

"Dew," she said, "but that bloody hip hurts."

The ghosts took no notice. They were beyond such concerns, and in that small way, she envied them. In her youth, she'd been a podium dancer in a Cardiff nightclub. The money had been good and the lifestyle glamorous—there had been no shortage of handsome suitors willing to spend a bob or two to impress her—but now she bore the insistent aches and pains that came from a life spent mostly on her feet (and quite often on her back).

With a chuckle, she remembered a week spent in a hotel with a couple of American seamen. She'd had eleven pounds in her purse and a Mexican stiletto concealed in the top of her nylon stocking. She'd also had a lump of hashish the size of a walnut pushed into her bra. She'd spent five days and four nights with the sailors and slept with both of them. They did her together, from opposite ends of the bed. They liked to watch each other having sex, but they needed a woman in the middle to keep things seemly. They wanted her straddled between them like a flesh condom so they could keep kidding themselves they weren't gay. Not that she minded. She had kind of a thing for pretty queer boys in uniform. All they had to do was give her enough whiskey, and she was happy to let them skewer her all night long. . . .

She sighed.

Those had been the days. Much as she'd loved her brother and life at the old lighthouse cottage, she'd never really acclimatized to the slower pace of life in Pontyrhudd. Her blood ran too hot. It always had. Even now, at the ridiculous age of ninety-two, she could feel it glowing in her veins like rocket fuel.

She settled her shoulders more comfortably against the pillow and thought of Alice.

The kids nowadays called her "Ragged Alice." She was the grey lady haunting their stories and inspiring them to dare one another to go up into the woods at night. But that hadn't always been the case. When Mrs. Phillips had known her, she was quite different. A slip of a thing, really, with a waist so narrow and cheeks so hollow it made her look eaten out from the inside. Back then, she'd simply been Mrs. Craig—a shaggy-haired, poetic beauty unhappily married to Bran Craig, a man with all the dynamism and romance of a fern.

Of course, the marriage had been one of convenience. Alice had already been three months pregnant when she walked down the aisle. And although most people assumed Holly to be Bran's daughter, Mrs. Phillips wasn't so sure. The airbase had still been open back then, and she'd heard rumours of local girls fraternising with the base personnel. And once or twice, she'd espied Alice slinking out of an evening, hair pinned up and lips slashed with scarlet. Was it beyond the realms of possibility to image the mooncalf had gotten herself knocked up by one of the flyboys and then convinced Bran to make an honest woman of her? Stranger things had happened in Pontyrhudd. Ieuan Davies had been responsible for a fair few unwanted pregnancies in his time. And now it turned out he'd also had a bit of a thing for muscular young tradesmen, God rest his prurient soul.

Mrs. Phillips chuckled to herself. Over the years, many so-called respectable people had looked down their nose at her. She'd been called a tart and worse. But towns like Pontyrhudd were like anthills. You never knew what secrets would be uncovered when you kicked them over.

Rain rattled against the sash window. A thin draft insinuated its way through a gap in the frame and stirred the net curtain.

Alice Craig had been killed shortly after the birth of her first daughter, and the killer had never been found. And now, thirty years later, people were being murdered again.

The knowledge had cast a pall over the town. Kids weren't allowed to play out on the streets. Curtains were drawn and doors locked. Even the ghosts seemed more subdued than normal.

Mrs. Phillips yawned. She loved a good mystery as much as the next person. But the schnapps had made her sleepy.

She yawned again and let her thoughts drift back through the decades to those long-gone Cardiff nights when she'd been a dancer surrounded by eager young men (and a lady or two).

Slowly, the thoughts turned to dreams and her breaths to snores.

When she awoke a few hours later, it was to find a black-clad figure standing at the end of her bed—a girl with chisel-sharp cheekbones and twigs in her eyes.

19.

THE SEARCH FOR CONSTABLE Perkins continued throughout the day. But by midafternoon, Holly's knee hurt so much she retired to her hotel room and ordered a bag of ice from the reception desk. The ice took down some of the swelling, and the painkillers took the edge off the worst of the discomfort, but she'd been overdoing things and she knew it. The only course of action that made any sense was to stay on her bed with her leg propped up on pillows and make sure she got some rest. But she didn't want to rest. Detective Superintendent Srivastava had made it pretty clear this case would determine the future trajectory of Holly's career. She had to find the killer, or she'd find herself rotated back into uniform, where they wouldn't tolerate her unconventional dress sense, burgeoning drink problem and generally insubordinate approach.

Damn whoever it was who had run her off the road. Damn them to hell! If she got her hands on them, they'd be limping too by the time they saw the inside of a cell. And if it turned out to have been Perkins, the idiot wouldn't know what had hit him. She smiled as she imagined smacking him in the head with her aluminium crutch. Wrapping it around his scrawny neck.

God, she could do with a drink.

She looked up at the nicotine-textured ceiling. She hadn't wanted to go back to her grandfather's house. She needed to be close to the incident room. If her team received news of Perkins, she'd rather be on site and able to hobble downstairs than reliant on Scott to come and collect her in his car. And besides, staying at the hotel had the added advantage of room service.

Using the seventies-style rotary phone on the nightstand, she called down to order a bottle of whiskey. If she was going to be stuck here in pain, she'd rather be drunk than brooding. That way, she might actually get some sleep.

When Sylvia arrived a few minutes later, the girl bore a tray carrying a half bottle of Penderyn single malt, a lone tumbler, and a small ceramic jug of water. She placed it beside the phone and straightened up.

"Is it still raining?" Holly asked.

"It is." Sylvia pulled her cardigan about her and scowled at the closed curtains. "And mark my words, no good will come of it."

"Come of what, the rain?"

"The weather's as unsettled as everything else. The

sooner this whole business gets sorted, the happier I'll be." She unscrewed the whiskey and poured a generous measure into the glass. Then a thought occurred to her. "Oh yes," she said, and rummaged in her cardigan pocket. "Here, somebody left a note for you."

Holly took the folded square of paper and opened it. Inside, the message consisted of four words made up of letters cut from newspaper headlines.

GET OUT OF PONTYRHUDD

The words were stark and anonymous, and unmistakably threatening. Holly's knee gave a twinge of pain. She fought down the memory of headlights advancing in her rearview mirror. "Do you know who left this?"

"I don't, I'm afraid." Sylvia held the whiskey glass out to Holly. "It was on the doormat this morning. Noticed it when I went to get the milk in, I did. Why, what's it say?"

Holly scrunched the paper into a ball. "Nothing of any consequence."

Sylvia shrugged. "Oh, well, in that case I'll be leaving you to your drink."

She turned to depart, but before she could, Mrs. Phillips shouldered into the room. The old woman looked distraught. Her hair was a mess and she'd obviously been sleeping in her clothes.

"I know who's doing it," she cried. "I know the killer. And they're not going to stop."

Sylvia stepped forward. "Come on, now, Mrs. Phillips. Don't go bothering the inspector." She tried to take her arm, but the old woman shook her off. Her rheumy eyes were wide and her makeup smudged.

"Listen," she said. "Just listen to me."

Holly elbowed herself into a sitting position. "What is it?"

Mrs. Phillips swallowed. Her skin looked like wax. "Your mother. The people who killed her." She staggered against the wardrobe. "They're not going to stop . . ."

The old woman's eyes rolled up into their sockets and she slid down the polished wood, onto the floor.

"Shit." Holly tried to swing her legs off the bed. "Is she okay?"

Sylvia knelt and cupped a hand over the old woman's mouth and nose. "She's still breathing."

"I'll call an ambulance."

"No, she wouldn't want that. She's just had one of her turns. It's happened before."

"Are you sure?"

"Of course I'm sure. A good night's sleep and hearty breakfast, and the old battle-axe will be right as rain, you'll see."

On the floor, Mrs. Phillips let out a slurred moan.

"Hoy," she quavered in a sleeper's voice, with her eyes still shut and her cheek still resting on the bare wooden floorboards. "Mind who you're calling an 'old battle-axe.'"

. . .

Despite her reassurances, Sylvia called the local GP, who came to attend Mrs. Phillips the following morning. From her bed, Holly could hear them talking through the thin wall.

"Now then." The doctor had the kind of deep, comfortable voice Holly associated with bearded old men in black-and-white British movies—a voice that conjured up images of pipes and tweed and inspired instant trust. "What's all this about, now, Ethel? Feeling a touch under the weather, are we?"

"Fuck off."

The doctor chuckled. "Nothing wrong with that tongue of yours, I see."

"I'm perfectly fine, thank you."

"That's not what I heard."

"And what is it you heard?"

"That you took a bit of a tumble last night."

"I may have tripped."

"Sylvia says you fainted."

"Ah, bollocks. That's just herself making a fuss. All that

happened was I ate a bad egg, that's all."

"Do you remember any of it?"

"Oh, get on with you. There's nothing to remember. I woke up feeling a bit hungover, and tripped over a rug."

"You'd been drinking?"

"Of course I'd been bloody drinking. I'm ninety-two years old! Why the fuck wouldn't I?"

Holly heard the doctor sigh.

"Have it your way, Ethel. Just maybe try cutting down on the booze and cigars, all right?"

"Get fucked."

"Fair play." The floorboards creaked. "I'll be off, then. Call me if you need anything."

"I won't be needing anything from you." Mrs. Phillips coughed. "I won't be dying in bed, see. When I go, I'll be somewhere they're playing loud music, I'll be surrounded by young men, and I'll have a glass of champagne in my hand."

20.

SCOTT CAME TO SEE Holly. He was carrying two paper cups with plastic lids. He perched on the side of the bed and wrinkled his nose. She was still wearing the same clothes she'd been wearing yesterday. Her mouth felt like a strip of old carpet, and she realised she probably stank of the previous evening's whiskey.

"All right, guv?" His gaze glanced off the empty bottle on the tray beside the bed.

"Any news on Perkins?"

"Not as yet. If he's done a runner, he's covered his tracks pretty well." He glanced down at her knee resting on its pillow. "How about you? Feeling any better?"

Holly shrugged. "It is what it is."

She wriggled her legs away from him. She wasn't used to having men she hardly knew sitting on the edge of her bed.

Apparently oblivious to her discomfort, Scott handed across one of the large cups.

"I brought you a cup of tea." From the pocket of his coat, he produced a couple of little plastic pots of cream and six sachets of brown sugar. "I thought you might need it."

Holly's tension evaporated. She pried off the plastic lid and inhaled the steam.

"Thank you."

"You're welcome." He watched her empty all the sugars and one of the creams into the brew. As usual, he'd left his coffee black and unsweetened. They sat sipping in companionable silence for a few moments.

Eventually, Holly said, "If I were a local cop turned serial killer, where would I hide?"

Scott sucked his bottom lip. "People would recognise him anywhere he went."

"Only if he stayed in town."

"So we're wasting our time looking for him?"

"Not at all." Holly scratched her inner forearm. She hadn't been able to go outside for a cigarette since the previous evening, and the tea had sparked a fierce craving.

"But if he's left town . . ."

"I don't think he has."

"What makes you say that?"

Holly shrugged. "Just a feeling."

Scott put down his coffee. "I'm here to learn," he said. "If there's more to your theory than just a hunch, I'd appreciate you sharing."

Holly looked down at her cup. She picked a scrap of fluff from the blanket covering her legs.

"Fair enough." She drew herself up and stretched her shoulders. "First off, I don't think he's finished. Whatever he's been trying to achieve with these killings, I don't think he's done it yet."

"You think he'll kill again? Why?"

"It's the manner of death," Holly said. "At first, I thought these killings might be retribution for the death of Lisa Hughes. Perkins finds her on the road, then goes after her boyfriend, then the lover of the man who impregnated her, and finally the mayor himself."

"That makes sense to me."

"But why mutilate the bodies in that way? Why copy a murder that happened when he was a very small boy?" She shook her head. "No, whatever's going on here, it's more than revenge for a hit-and-run. These people were killed for a purpose, and those exact injuries—the spikes in the eyes and the slit across the abdomen—are all part of it."

"And then there's the connection to the airbase, and your mother's murder."

"I hadn't forgotten about that."

Scott stood, and Holly eased herself to the edge of the bed. "Pass my crutch, would you?"

"Where are we going?"

"Downstairs."

Slowly and uncomfortably, with one hand on the banister and the other on her crutch, she negotiated the steep wooden stairs. Scott tried to help, but she shook him off. She knew he meant well, but she was in too much pain to be manhandled.

By the time they reached the incident room, her jaw ached from being clenched, and she was relived to find the room empty. Apparently everyone else was out searching for Perkins.

Someone had left a chair in front of her whiteboard. She levered herself into it.

By now, the board was a mess of scribbled notes, with arrows connecting the various victims. The newest arrows had been left last night, before she retired to her room. These were thick black lines linking the three youngest victims and Perkins to the local school.

"Did we hear back from the school?"

Scott perched on the edge of the table beside her. "Yes, we sent one of the uniforms up there this morning. Their records confirm all four were in the same year, the same as their parents were."

"What?"

"All their parents were in the same year at school."

The hairs prickled on the back of Holly's neck. Something fluttered in her chest. She couldn't decide if she was excited, or on the verge of an anxiety attack.

"What about the mayor?"

"Davies?" Scott pulled out his phone. "I'll check."

Despite the tea, Holly's mouth had gone dry. "And check my mother, too."

Scott thought about it, and his eyes widened as the penny dropped. "Could that be the connection?"

Holly gave a shrug. She didn't know. But the blood sang in her veins with the anticipation of finding a solution.

"The sooner you get on to the school," she said, "the sooner we'll find out."

Her gaze lit on the photographs she'd been given in the pub. Her fingertips rearranged them on the tabletop. Those images from thirty years ago. Whatever was going on, *that* had been the moment it all started, with her mother and the experiment.

"Holy fuck," she said.

Scott looked around. "Are you okay?"

"Yeah, I . . . I think I know where we'll find Perkins."

. . .

They left the car on the edge of the road and made their way on foot down the muddy track that led to the river. Holly's crutch kept sinking into the soft ground, but each time she stumbled, Scott was there to catch her elbow.

The wind shook the trees. Echoing up the valley came the sound of surf striking the beach. Flecks of rain prefigured an oncoming deluge.

Eventually, they came to the place where Holly's mother had died. A small bridge, little more than a mossy old railway sleeper, led them over the water where Holly had almost drowned to the stone circle sitting on its little boggy promontory.

As Holly had suspected, Constable Perkins stood waiting. His face looked pinched and pale, and his clothes were wet to the chest, as if he'd waded through the reddish waters to reach this spot. He had been standing to one side of the stones, apparently gazing downstream. But as they approached, he turned to face them. In his shivering hand, he carried a silver-plated carving knife.

"Go away," he said.

Holly shook her head. "Sorry, pal. You know that's not going to happen."

The constable raised a bony finger. "You shouldn't be here."

The man's soul flickered and squirmed behind his eyes as light and dark writhed against each other like eels in a tank. Holly had never seen anything like it. And yet, something about the darkness in his head called to her. Something about it felt almost familiar. . . .

21.

ALICE LEANT AGAINST THE TREE. *The roughness of the bark pressed into her shoulders through the thin cotton of her summer dress, and she felt a delicious thrill as she sparked a cigarette. Her husband didn't approve of her smoking. He didn't approve of a lot of things she did. But then, tonight wasn't about him. Tonight she wasn't a wife or a mother. Tonight, no matter how queasy she might feel at the thought of abandoning her little family, she was simply Alice. And she had the whole of the rest of her life ahead of her.*

As soon as Martin was done guarding whatever the boffins were doing in the woods, he'd come and find her and take her back to the base with him. And then tomorrow, they'd be on the early train to Birmingham. By the time her husband realised she wasn't coming home, they'd be well on the way to Martin's new posting in Kent. And once they had settled into the married quarters, they could send for little Holly. After all, she was their daughter. She'd been conceived in the back of an RAF Land Rover one night last year.

She sucked smoke into her chest. The sky overhead was

pale with the last light of the day, but here beneath the trees it was already dark.

"I'm doing the right thing," she said, trying to reassure the nervous and excited butterflies flittering in her chest.

And that was when she heard them coming.

At first, her heart leapt, thinking Martin had come to find her. Then she realised the footsteps were coming from the wrong direction. Instead of coming from the river, they were approaching from the road. And they weren't alone. She heard low voices. Saw torchlight flickering through the undergrowth.

She dropped the cigarette to the leaf-strewn floor and ground it out with her foot.

Shit.

The last thing she needed was to be discovered now.

She edged around the trunk until she was on the opposite side, with only the river behind her. But the voices grew closer, seemingly making directly for this spot.

Should she run?

If she left now, Martin might think she'd lost her nerve. He might leave tomorrow without her, and the thought of being stuck in Pontyrhudd without him was intolerable.

Besides, if she moved now, they'd hear her. They were getting that close. Screwing her eyes shut, she pushed herself up against the tree's rough bark, willing it to swallow her.

As the sound of footsteps entered the little clearing, she

held her breath. Her heart seemed to be trying to punch its way out through her ribs.

No, *she thought.* Not now. Not when I'm so close . . .

Someone shone a torch in her face. Rough hands grabbed her and pulled her away from the tree.

She blinked against the darkness, her vision still swimming from the glare of the torch.

"Well, well, well," *a familiar voice said.* "What do we have by here?"

"Davies?"

"You can call me Ieuan, love."

"What the fuck do you want?" *Ieuan Davies had been in the year above her at school. She remembered him as a petty little thug with delusions of grandeur.*

He laughed. "Me and the boys here come with a message."

Holly's eyes had started to adjust. In the torchlight, she recognised Davies's cronies and former classmates: Jim Perkins and Owen the meat—a pair of proper morons with hardly a brain cell between them.

"What message?"

Davies's lip curled. "That we don't like the RAF boys, see? We don't like the way they crack onto our local girls."

"Why are you telling me?"

"Because you're up here to meet one, aren't you?"

"No."

"Yes, you are. My old man heard Steve Woodrow talking

about it in the pub. Said he knew you got knocked up by one of those bastards."

Alice looked around. She had her back to the river and nowhere to go. Where was Martin?

In the direction of the stone circle, blue lightning danced soundlessly between the trees.

"I don't want no trouble," she said.

Davies's sneer turned into a smirk. "It don't matter what you want." He held a hand to Owen and the lad passed him a knife. "As I told you, we're here to send a message."

22.

"**PUT THE KNIFE DOWN.**" Scott held out a warning hand. "Just put it down and we can talk about this."

Perkins ignored him. His attention remained fixed on Holly.

"Please," he said. "I don't want you to see me like this."

"Then put the knife down."

"I can't." Perkins looked suddenly stricken. "I haven't finished yet."

In the corner of her vision, Holly saw Scott inching forwards. She spoke to keep Perkins focused on her.

"Finished what?"

"I have a list. Davies, Owen . . ."

"What about Daryl Allen."

"Who?"

"The fellow you left in the graveyard with his guts hanging out."

"Oh, him." Perkins shrugged. "He was a favour for a friend."

"What friend?"

"Lisa Hughes. She's the reason I'm here. Her death's

what kicked this all off again."

Scott had sidled almost within striking distance. Barely taking his eyes from Holly, Perkins lunged with the knife. Scott tried to deflect the attack with his forearm, but the momentum of the thrust pushed his parry aside, and he cried out as the blade sank into his stomach, a few inches above and to the left of his navel.

Holly tried to intervene, but she was too slow on her crutch. Before she'd managed to take more than a step, Perkins was facing her again, holding the blood-greased knife at arm's length.

"Please don't come any closer," he said.

Scott sat with his back against one of the stones. His face had turned deathly white, but he had both hands clamped over the entry wound in his midsection. Thick, dark blood oozed between his fingers. His feet squirmed in the mud.

"You have to stop this." Holly blinked away mental images of the injured kids at Hawk Road Primary School. "This man needs medical attention."

Perkins gave a snort. "I warned him to leave. He should have listened."

"Was he on your list?"

The man's expression faltered. "No."

"Then you don't have to let him die. You could help me to help him."

"Why should I? Nobody was there to help me when I needed it."

Holly took a deep breath. She was sure she could use her crutch as a weapon if she had to, although that would leave her dangerously off-balance.

"So what are you going to do?" she asked. "Are you going to try to kill me, too?"

Perkins's eyes widened. "No!"

"Then give me the knife."

"I can't. Not yet. I still have one person left on my list."

"Who?"

Perkins pressed the tip of his knife to the underside of his jaw. "This guy."

"No."

"He's the last on my list. I owe his dad that much, at least."

Holly hobbled towards him. "No."

"I'm just glad I got to see you again."

"What do you mean?"

"I always wondered how you'd turn out."

Perkins took a firm two-handed grip on the handle. He was going to push the knife up through his soft palate and into his brain, and Holly didn't think she could close the distance between them in time to prevent it.

"Stop!" The voice came from the bridge. Holly turned to see Mrs. Phillips striding towards them in a black silk ball gown, with mud on her hem and a thunderous expression on her face. Amy Lao hurried to keep up with her.

"Stop this at once," Mrs. Phillips said. She jabbed a gnarled root of a finger at Perkins. "What *do* you think you're doing?"

"Go away," Perkins said. "This doesn't concern you."

"Oh, but it does!" The old woman drew herself up. "Because I know exactly who you are."

"So?"

"So release poor Neil, and stop this foolishness."

Holly tried to intervene, but the old woman would not be deflected. Lao rolled her eyes and shrugged.

The knife lowered a fraction. "If you know who I am," Perkins said, "you know why I have to do this."

Mrs. Phillips made a face. "Alice, you don't *have* to do anything."

"Do you know what those bastards did?"

"I do, but you aren't making things any better. Not really. And do you think your daughter wants to see you push a carving knife through Neil Perkins's noddle? I don't think she does. Poor lamb's seen enough already."

Perkins turned his eyes to Holly. They were wide now, and glistening.

"I'm sorry," he said. The knife fell from his fingers and implanted itself tip-first into the soft ground. "I'm so sorry."

Holly moved forward and pulled a pair of cuffs from her jacket pocket. She had some difficulty securing Perkins's wrists one-handed, but the man didn't struggle.

When he was securely trussed and kneeling on the ground a safe distance from the knife that still protruded from the grass like an Arthurian sword, Holly sent Lao to raise the alarm. Then she turned to Mrs. Phillips.

"What the fuck was all that about?"

But the old lady had collapsed, and only the crows in the trees could provide any answer.

23.

AFTER THE FUNERAL, HOLLY sat in the car at the kerb outside the hotel.

"Are you sure you're all right to drive?" Scott asked for the fifth time since they'd seen Mrs. Phillips laid to rest beside her brother.

"I'm fine sitting down," Holly replied, tapping her hands against the steering wheel. "I only use my ankles on the pedals. No weight on my knee at all."

Scott was wearing one of his suits. A black one, with a navy shirt and a silver tie, which flapped in the sea breeze. Beneath the shirt his knife wound had been cleaned and stitched. He would be stiff and sore for some time but expected to make a full recovery. Lao stood beside him in a black dress with matching pillbox hat and veil.

"What are you going to say in your report?" she asked.

Holly shrugged. "What is there to say? Constable Perkins was in love with Lisa Hughes. When she was killed, he suffered some sort of psychotic break. He killed Daryl for obvious reasons. Then killed Mike Owen in order to get to Ieuan Davies, because he knew

Davies and Hughes had had an affair."

"Simple as that?"

"As simple as that."

"And what about all that stuff about your mother?"

"Everybody in Pontyrhudd knows about Ragged Alice. It's not surprising he'd latch on to the story."

"So, nothing to do with those photographs Woodrow gave you?"

Holly shook her head. She was anxious to get on the road back to Carmarthen. "The man's an acid casualty," she said. "Probably a conspiracy theorist, too."

Lao looked unconvinced, but Scott seemed satisfied. Holly smiled at him. "It's been good working with you," she said.

He looked surprised but tried to cover it. "Good to work with you, too, guv."

"Maybe I'll see you again."

"I'd like that."

Holly turned the ignition and he stepped back. She gave Lao a final wink and pulled away. Scott raised a hand in farewell, but Lao continued waving madly as Holly traversed the entire length of the seafront.

Then she was through the town and climbing up the valley, away from the sea and the shadow of the lighthouse, letting Pontyrhudd fall away behind her like a shed skin. As the car emerged from the shadow of the valley and the bright afternoon sun dappled the dashboard, she felt a stirring at the back of her head.

"Are you okay in there, Mam?" she asked.

"I've been in worse places." Alice spoke without speaking, her words manifesting in Holly's mind without troubling her ears. "Thank you for taking me with you. I thought I'd never get away from those blasted stones."

"You're welcome."

They rode in companionable silence for a few minutes, until they reached the junction with the main road. Holly looked both ways, as if trying to decide which direction to turn the wheel. The pub called to her with the promise of temporary oblivion, but she chose to ignore it. With a sigh, she turned right, towards Carmarthen and home.

"So," Alice said. "What happens now?"

Holly gripped the steering wheel and stared at the main road unwinding away ahead of them.

"Honestly, Mam," she said, "I have no idea."

About the Author

Tom Shot Photography

GARETH L. POWELL is the author of five science fiction novels and two short story collections. His third novel, *Ack-Ack Macaque,* book one in the Macaque Trilogy, was the winner of the 2013 BSFA novel award. He lives in Bristol, UK.

TOR·COM

Science fiction. Fantasy. The universe.

And related subjects.

*

More than just a publisher's website, *Tor.com* is a venue for **original fiction, comics,** and **discussion** of the entire field of SF and fantasy, in all media and from all sources. Visit our site today—and join the conversation yourself.